Home

BY
LISA ALLEN-AGOSTINI

First published in Great Britain by Papillote Press in 2018

A CIP catalogue record for this book is available from the British Library

Typeset in Minion

Printed by CPI Group (UK) Ltd, Croydon CR0 4YY

Book cover and design by Andy Dark

ISBN: 978-1-9997768-3-1

Papillote Press
23 Rozel Road
London SW4 0EY
United Kingdom,
and Trafalgar, Dominica
www.papillotepress.co.uk
@papillotepress

To the memory of my parents, Rito and Dolsie

Chapter

1

That sound; that burbling, bubbling sound. That ringtone was possibly the most annoying sound in the whole world. But it was my lifeline to home.

I hit the big green button. Akilah's face popped up on my screen. She whispered, "Hey, you. What's going on?" Akilah was in church clothes, dolled up with a prim little cardigan over a modest dress. I could just see the collar and buttons below said face. Said face was rushing out of the church as we spoke. Her mom would eat that up. Yet another reason to hate the reviled best friend: I made Akilah leave church while the service was going on.

All these thoughts rushed through me in between the spasms of terror I felt. Those clutching, needle-sharp pains in my stomach had started and before I dissolved into a puddle of tears and snot I'd had the good sense to send Akilah a Skype message: "Not doing so great. Be nice to talk."

What can I say? I have a rare gift for understatement.

Lucky for me she had her phone on—a no-no as far as her mom was concerned. "Phones off in church" was a strict rule. Lucky for me Akilah knew I was having a hard time and had defied her mother to be there for me. Lucky for me, she was a great friend.

She was my best friend—and she was my only friend.

"God," I groaned. "Ki-ki, I'm dying."

"No, girl, you're not dying," she responded. She was whispering and walking at the same time; and I could see that where she was the sunlight was blinding. "Now, what's the matter?"

"Nothing," I said. "Everything."

"That's not an answer," she told me. "What is causing you to feel like this right now?" She was familiar with my panic attacks: I'd get sweaty, my heart would race, I'd feel breathless and terrified and end up sobbing for hours. It wasn't a good look. What amazed me was that she was always ready to give me a shoulder to cry on. Before I'd got to Canada, hers was the only one I had.

I explained my situation: I was walking to the bus stop, trying to get home.

I took another step on the long white highway, Akilah's quiet, sure voice talking to me, telling me, *You will get there, you will not get lost, you will find the bus station, you will catch a bus, you will get home.*

It was about seventeen degrees, warm for Canadians but cold for me; I haven't got used to the weather yet. For them it's a nice day, and they put on shorts and tank tops and walk around like I would at the beach or in the park but for me, it's just another wrap-up-tight day, wear-my-coat day, feel-too-cold day. Home was never this cold, even on the chilliest nights, even up in the high hills where mist covers the road in the early morning.

I felt the wind blowing through my short, black hair, trying to ruffle it and failing. *Canadian wind, oh you don't know anything about hair like mine. You haven't seen enough of it in this quiet backwoods on the prairie. You think my hair is gonna just submit to you, flip and dance in you, fly and move in you? Not my hair. It's worked too hard for too long to just give in to you. It's tough hair, wiry hair, strong hair, hair that won't be cowed by some damn prairie wind. No siree, not this hair.*

"Sweetie, are you there?" Akilah asked sharply.

When I'm having a panic attack I can find it hard to carry a conversation. My thoughts become confused and all the words become tangled in my mind, a ball of stifled self-expression. So I tried to focus on the road I was walking on.

A long concrete road, it was four lanes wide and full of zooming, beeping, clanking, whooshing cars, buses and trucks. Trucks especially.

The trucks were big, lumbering, trundling things that passed too close to me as I walked. The pavement and road were the same colour, the same texture. Roads back home were black, the way roads should be. This bone white, cold concrete scared me in some primal way. This wasn't a road into anything good; it couldn't be. And the trucks were like huge devils with horns blaring and fangs in their grills, evil grins, bad intentions, bearing down on me from behind, leering at me from the other side of the road as they powered past, warning me they'd be back for me—not now but at some unspecified, very real date in the future. The wind they raised was bitter and hot, not like the normal wind in the city of Edmonton that blows cold, odourless and sterile. The wind from the sides of the trucks was dusty, like ashes in my mouth.

Houses ran alongside the road. Stretching over the four lanes every now and then was a big blue road sign that told me where I was. I was also keeping track by counting the street signs at each corner. Twenty-first Street. Twentieth Street. Nineteenth Street. The streets seemed inordinately far apart. I had four more blocks to walk before I turned into the bus station.

"What's going on, though?" Akilah was now insistent. "Why are you walking in the middle of nowhere?"

"I should take a bus to the station, then from the station to home," I confessed to her. "But I never remember quickly enough which bus

3

to take to get to the station. I feel like an idiot standing there staring at the transit map. I keep some schedules in my pocket, but..."

It sounds stupid, but I was always, always easily confused. *Rice or pasta? Lettuce or cabbage? The Seventeen or the Eighteen?* And please don't get me started on multiple-choice tests. Exams were always hell. I never knew how to decide things. So instead of trying to decide which bus to take, I walked to the little bus station, with its heavy, warm air panting out of buses that crouched in a waiting lane, engines still running. Meanwhile the drivers used the bathroom or made phone calls to their families, or just shot the breeze with other workers in the small office behind the bulletproof glass of the customer service counter.

The bus schedules in my pocket, clutched too tight too many times, had become grimy and old through the weeks I'd used them. No matter how many times I took the bus, I always forgot which one I needed.

Having a panic disorder really sucks.

If I sat and took really deep breaths, I could remember that mornings my bus was the Fourteen, going north into the city; and evenings my bus was the Eighteen, going south into the suburbs. But when I was in the grip of a panic attack there was no way I could remember that, as ridiculous as it might sound. I had to pull out both schedules every time I walked to catch a bus. I had to smooth out the wrinkles, squint down at them and look to see which bus went where. And as soon as I put them back into my pocket I forgot again. *Which bus goes where? What time is it running? Am I in the right place?*

"You're not an idiot," Akilah consoled me. "In fact, you're one of the smartest people I know. Everybody says so."

"Meh," I said dismissively. "So smart I can't remember which bus to take to get home. Every. Single. Day."

She laughed.

"Could you just talk to me?" I begged. "Tell me what's going on with school and church and everything. How did you do in end of term test?"

As Akilah, recognising my strategy as one of distraction, started talking, I noticed the breeze even more. This afternoon wind seemed determined to get to me, to find something it could ruffle. It crept under my jeans and under my high collar, trying to penetrate the layers of fabric to reach my skin. I could feel it swirling under my clothes. But I was prepared, too wily for the wind. I had on long underwear.

I was a bit closer to the bus station. Listening to Akilah's voice was calming me down. I could pay attention to small things again, like the flowers in front of people's houses, or the faint warmth of the sunshine on my face.

Summer in Edmonton is not hot, but it's not cold. Unless, that is, you're used to living in a furnace. I was.

I am from the Caribbean, where an average day might easily be twice as hot as an average Edmonton summer day. What is sixteen degrees when you're really built for thirty-two? So I was always cold, bundling myself up in layers and obscenely more layers, wearing all the clothes in my wardrobe at once.

Aunt Jillian and Julie laughed at me all the time. They couldn't understand why I was always kitted out like a bag lady in sweater, shirt, long underwear, jeans and sneakers. On really bad days I wore my coat, a long velveteen number I bought at a thrift store because I wasn't going to be in this city much longer and I was too ashamed to ask for a more expensive one. I figured nobody wanted to spend real money on my "penance" clothes. My velveteen coat is a rich, electric blue, the colour of the sky at home when it is just about sunset—not on the side with the lightshow of the sun going down in an orange blaze of glory but the other one, the side where night is creeping up and day is already a memory. The sky could be such an elegant, intense, impenetrable and unutterably lovely blue. When I saw the coat on the hanger, it seemed it was waiting for me. Everybody laughed at me, especially Julie, who called it my Princess Di coat. In truth it was too formal for everyday use but I didn't care. It fitted me and I loved the colour and the smooth, short nap of the velveteen. The lining was real silk, which was heavenly against my skin.

Plus when you're wearing a big, thick coat it feels like it's easy to disappear.

I kept walking, making a fist with my free hand and sticking it into the silk-lined pocket. My short nails pressed pink crescents into my palm, the pain keeping me from screaming out when the scary trucks passed with their *boooohhhhhppp!* Horns blaring. Devil trucks.

"Nobody ever stops me or says hello or anything," I suddenly said to Akilah. "I'm walking here and nobody says a word. Canadians are so into their own space that they try not to interfere with anybody else's."

Akilah, used to my disjointed thoughts during my panic attacks, picked up the ball and ran with it. "Not like the *macos* we have here in Trinidad," she teased. "Always macoing your business. Aunty Cynthia would have got about three phone calls by now if you were home and walking down the highway."

It was true, sort of. At home, people stop and talk to perfect strangers. At least you'd smile at them and see in their faces some human emotion. Here, a strange and hostile silence fell when the occasional person came towards me. Not that I saw too many people on this walk.

"Nobody walks here," I told her. "I'm a freak," I moaned. "Aunty Jillian and her girlfriend would have picked me up from the city if I had asked them to, but that would have meant them driving out of their way." I bit my lip. "I don't want to be too much trouble."

"Oh, sweetie," Akilah sighed.

"Well, they don't work in the city! They work from home, so they would have to leave home, pick me up and drive all the way back. I don't want to be a nuisance."

I was being dishonest. Yes, they did work from home. They had a computer-based business that they ran from the cool, dry basement of their little house in the suburbs. But I knew they would have been happy to pick me up from the city. I told myself maybe things would change once I got more used to being in Edmonton, that maybe I wouldn't feel like such a burden, crashing in and ruining their perfect lives while I served out my penance here. Maybe.

It was nearly summer. School was out. Trying to make myself invisible I spent my days at the library, reading; I liked books, probably because I spent so much time alone with them when I was little. Sometimes I went to the gym. Sometimes I went swimming. Sometimes I went to the museum. Sometimes I just walked around the city and listened to it breathe.

I was officially in Edmonton on holiday, recovering from my recent *troubles*. My mom had shunted me off here. I was half-a-world away from home to hide for the rest of the school term that I had started by trying to kill myself.

It was now June and I was tired of my penance.

Why did I call it penance? Because my mother was so ashamed of my suicide attempt and my mental illness, when she sent me away to recover it felt like she was punishing me: so penance.

Penance was hard. I missed the sunshine, I missed my room, I missed my house, I missed Akilah. I did not miss school. And I didn't miss my mother as much as I should but then every time I thought of her I remembered the sour and hurt expression on her face, the first thing I saw when I came to at the hospital. She couldn't believe that I was so unhappy that I wanted to die. She felt it was a personal indictment of her and my upbringing. It was clinical depression, I tried to tell her, the doctors tried to tell her, Aunt Jillian tried to tell her. Depression is an illness. It had nothing to do with her. It was inside of me, like some kind of glitch in my basic programming. My operating software told my body I was unhappy and that I wanted to die. It didn't matter if she was a good mother or not. I would have taken the bottle of pills anyway.

I was still walking. Akilah was still on Skype, but she warned me she would have to go soon. "Mummy will kill me if I don't go back inside." Sure enough, I heard Aunty Patsy's sharp high heels clicking on the church steps and her stern voice telling Akilah to get back to the service. We ended the call.

I could breathe again. The road wasn't so terrifying anymore.

The summer flowers outside each house on this road were brighter than I would have imagined when I was living in the Caribbean. I had always imagined Canada—or any temperate place, actually—as dull and somehow less colourful than home. I had been surprised to see that the flowers could be as red, as yellow and as blue as the flowers in my own garden. Not knowing the names of anything, I called them by their sizes, shapes, and colours: the big pink flower, the small blue flower, the orange flower with the dizzy, swirling petals. The wind had more success with them than with my wiry, tight curls. Those flowers danced in it, their little heads nodding and twisting in the strong breeze.

Once, before I got the courage to take the bus at all, I tried walking straight home from the city. Twenty-four blocks didn't seem like much—and it only took about fifteen minutes by car to get from the heart of town to my aunt's house, so I figured I could get away with walking it. Uh uh. It was *long*. In fact, in my mind I called it *The Day of the Longest Walk*. I walked for about three hours and just kept counting streets and counting streets until in frustration I stopped a little kid and asked did he know where Second Street was?

Turned out I was actually standing on it, right in front of Aunt Jillian's house. The houses all looked exactly the same to me and I just hadn't recognised it. But there it was: a small, brownish-white cottage surrounded by a perfect, jewel-green lawn and tubs of summer blooms, separated from its neighbours by a hedge and a chain-link fence. On one side of the house was a black-doored garage with an extra car parked outside on the driveway in front of it. Aunt Jillian had a couple of garden gnomes cavorting in a little grotto she had made of Japanese-looking rocks and stones, some dark green perennial shrub, and pieces of driftwood she had picked up from a beach back home. It was not a shrine, but she tended this grotto carefully, raking it and keeping it looking really nice, washing down the garden gnomes until they shone even though she made constant fun of them. I imagined they had secret lives like the singing gnomes in a movie I liked when I was a kid, *Gnomeo and Juliet*.

On *The Day of the Longest Walk*, I had been confused too because of perspective. I'd never seen Aunty Jillian's house from that angle. I had always driven up into the garage in the passenger seat of Aunt Jillian's car, and entered the house through the side door in the garage. Nobody used the front door at all, I noticed. Seemed it was only there for decoration. People entered through the back door into the kitchen or through the garage where a side door led to the hallway between the formal living room and the rest of the house. The front door was seldom even touched, except by Julie during her Saturday morning cleaning rampages, when every bit of brass and glass in the house was polished till it gleamed like new. The front door was formal and austere, like the living room into which it opened, and perhaps nobody wanted that feeling of formality to be sullied with ordinary dirt and cat fur and Doritos smudges.

I turned a corner, counting streets laterally this time. I knew the street names by heart now, and ran through them in my head as if I were afraid someone might have secretly changed them in the night just to confuse me. In my mind I called their names as I passed them: Fir, Pine, Aspen—names of trees I didn't know from home at all— then the bus station came into view.

Two cops idly watched my approach. They were wearing summer uniforms of short sleeves and short pants, and looked with obvious amusement at my over-padded appearance. I smiled faintly at them and clenched my fists tighter in my pockets. It was a strange contradiction: I hated how nobody talked to me, but at the same time I didn't really want anybody to talk to me either. Maybe I was afraid of what I'd say in return. Or maybe I was afraid I'd just turn into a puddle of shame and terror right at their feet. Who knew?

The taller of the two cops, a very young blond guy with strong, thick legs, grinned back at my vague smile. As soon as I was in earshot he asked if I was sure I was warm enough. I said yes, thanks, and hearing my Caribbean accent he immediately did what every other white Canadian I'd ever met had done: he asked me where I was from.

Trinidad, I told him, escaping to the sheltered booth of the commuter queue, yearning to get my chilled bones out of the wind.

I quickly warmed up. I looked at my little watch, which my mother had given me three years ago when I sat my secondary school entrance exam. A practical present, of course, as you couldn't take the exam with a cell phone as your timer.

I had another ten minutes until the next bus would arrive. The bus service on this line ran every twenty minutes, waiting for no one a minute past the schedule. It was shocking to me at first to read the schedule and find that the buses actually would be there at nine-twenty if they said they would be; at home, no such thing had ever happened. In Trinidad, buses ran when their drivers felt like it, end of story. Schedules, if they existed, were mere suggestions, rather than rules. The majority of people took a kind of minibus we call a maxi-taxi, and those ran whenever they liked. But here, the bus drivers were always on time, like serious professionals, saying *goodmorningma'am* or *goodeveningsir* or whatever to every single person who came in. Miraculously, they asked nobody how their grandson was doing in school, or how their diabetes—in Trinidad we call it *sugar*—was treating them, or how their *macomere* was keeping. It didn't matter that I saw the same driver more often than not; his tone didn't change when he said *goodmorningma'am* every single morning and *goodafternoonma'am* every single evening.

Standing in the windbreak I could see the boyish-looking cop staring at me still and even though I turned away to look in the other direction I knew he would soon amble over to make small talk. So said, so done, and he came over, swinging his arms and rhythmically catching his fists together in front as he did. The gray and yellow of his uniform was different from what I expected of a policeman's; the jaunty yellow stripe was, I felt, unnecessarily frivolous, like a party hat on a pig. In my country the police are not friendly. They do not stop to shoot the breeze or *old talk* with anybody, especially teenage girls. Here, though, this cop came over and talked about the weather and the neighbourhood and then asked how old I was. I told him fourteen and he visibly took a mental step back and made some little excuse and quickly ambled back to his partner. I didn't know what had happened, or why. Humans are a mysterious species when you have a panic disorder. *Was he going to arrest me for truancy? Was he going to search me for drugs? Would he try to deport me as an illegal alien, even though I had my tourist visa?*

Oh, the crap that ran through my head. *Man*, I thought again, *having a panic disorder sucks.*

One of the purring buses in the small bullpen of the station suddenly emitted a little burst of wind, a sharp mechanical fart, and rumbled awake. It drove up to me and I anxiously checked my schedule once more. I was alone in the queue. When the bus reached me the door came open with a gasp. Despite the fact that the number was written plain as day on the front of the bus, I got on and asked was it the Eighteen. *Yup, goodafternoonma'am*, the driver said. I paid the fare, lurched to a seat in the middle of the bus and sat down gratefully on the cold, slippery vinyl. Another mechanical breaking of wind and we were off.

I counted the streets again, and then I was home. Not *home home*, I thought with a little wave of longing. Was this what *tabanca* was like? I'd never been homesick before, far less lovesick. But I pushed the feeling down. Home at Aunt Jillian's house was good enough for now. I reached up, pulled the stop cord and got out when the bus stopped rolling. The bus stop was a half-block from the house but I'd done it so many times it was hardly something I had to think about anymore. My anxieties were left on the bus, for now. And finally the penny dropped: the boyish cop had been flirting with me before he heard my age.

Chapter

2

I've never thought of myself as a pretty child, not the kind you'd look at and say, *Oh what a little angel!* or anything like that. My little face in baby pictures was too serious, and I think I grew up to be the kind of child adults admire because I'm smart and well-read, rather than because of how I looked. I was tall and skinny with dark brown skin and big black eyes that Akilah said made me look older than I was. Though I was shy, I had a good vocabulary, and when I used big words like I normally did adults acted like it was a trick I could do as if I were some kind of monkey dancing on a chain or a dog doing flips on command.

Adults always said to each other: *she's so articulate!* They would have this conversation with each other like I wasn't even there. And really, sometimes I wasn't. It came to be like I didn't really care what they said anymore. I was doing my thing, talking or writing or reading or whatever, and they would be admiring me like I was a fish in a bowl. And I didn't care, I just swam around in my dirty water and sucked up the stale food and my own pee—metaphorically speaking, of course—and everything was cool. Only, everything wasn't cool.

I was really, really unhappy, like I had this big hole in my belly between my heart and my stomach and I couldn't fill it with food or with love or books or anything and I just felt *sad*, all the time, all the time, all the time.

I must have always been that way. I remember that when I was really small, maybe like five or six years old, I picked up a knife to stab my mother after she scolded me for some reason. She denies this story, by the way. She says it never happened. But I remember the weight of the knife in my hand. I remember the rage and pain I felt because she had made me angry, and I remember thinking if I could hit her with that knife *hard hard hard* she would stop hurting me. And I remember too that she took the knife away from me and gave me some slaps on my bottom and I went to bed crying and I woke up later feeling, not for the first time and not for the last, that big pit.

The hole was bigger than me, sometimes, and when I woke up that day, the day after I tried to stab my mother, the hole was there, big and yawning and evil and hard and ugly. I hated myself for what I had done and I wished it were me I had tried to kill with that big shiny knife instead of my mother.

When I was *home home* I went to an ordinary school. Just like the thousands of other kids my age in my country, I wore a uniform that was ugly and designed to make me feel unimportant and like a sheep; no individuality allowed. My school wasn't big, or special, just a village school with ordinary teachers teaching ordinary stuff like English and maths and social studies, the name of the national flower, the population of the earth and stuff like that.

Akilah and I had been friends from the first day of kindergarten. We were the brightest kids in every class. Everybody thought we'd go from primary school to secondary school together. We didn't. When we both sat that secondary entrance exam, only one of us did well. Akilah went to a prestigious convent school where they taught French, not just English and Spanish. They didn't teach technical drawing or woodwork. It wasn't that kind of school. Mine was exactly the opposite.

School was so easy I was bored most of the time. Every year was the same thing. I would read the books twice before the start of term and know all the information and more because I had gone to the little library in town while waiting for my mother after school and looked up everything I wanted to know before it could come up in class. I read about women's rights, the Black Power movement, the Renaissance, the Harlem Renaissance… you name it, I'd read about it. The librarians smiled benignly at me every time I walked into the library with a stack of books fatter than I was myself. I was everything they had dreamed of: a bookish girl who would sit quietly, and methodically read everything they had on the fiction shelves and then start working through the Dewey decimal system of non-fiction titles. It was a small library and it didn't take me long to make my way through all the books I was even vaguely interested in.

Everybody thought I was smart.

Everybody except me.

Though I had read all of this stuff I wasn't conscious that I knew anything at all, and I've always thought of myself as kind of stupid. It didn't help that my panic disorder made me freak out every time I had a test. Like the numbers of the buses, everything I knew flew right out of my head when I got anxious. Anxiety starts as a little scared butterfly in the pit of my stomach and eventually grows into a giant, sweeping moth that destroys my ability to focus and recall what I know. I can't tell you how many times I've failed exams about things I know backwards and forwards.

The last test I sat at my old school was about geography. I knew all about clouds and fronts and the tides—but not one single useful fact stayed in my head during that test. Of course, I failed. I think back to that test and kick myself because I knew all the answers. Somehow I couldn't convince my brain that I did, not when the test was actually going on.

Honestly, I don't understand why this stuff happens to me. Why can't I just take a stupid test? Why do I feel so bad, ugly and stupid all the time? Why was everything about me just... *wrong*?

Take for instance my hair. For most of my life I wore my hair in short plaits, which my mother impatiently put in and took out on alternate weekends, taking about three hours each time she did them fresh. My hair wasn't long enough to reach my shoulders and in my country that's saying something. Everybody always said *a woman's hair is her glory* and if she has good grass growing up there it's an asset. I never did see the point. So what if some dead cuticle pushes out longer rather than shorter? Who cares? And then last year I cut it all off, without consulting my mother, and she hit the roof. But I like it better this way, almost clinging to my head, so short. I looked like a boy, my mother said, but I didn't care. It was my hair and if I wanted to cut it right off I would.

Besides, Aunt Jillian had short hair, I reminded her. Now, understand that my mother is as black as the ace of spades, just like me. For her to change colour is pretty tough. But she did it; I swear she turned pale. Aunt Jillian isn't someone I should take pattern from, she said, then clammed up and wouldn't say anything else.

Why not, I wanted to know. All my life she had pointed to her sister Jillian as a shining example of virtuous daughterhood, the one who had made good and made their sick mother proud before the woman's death. In Canada, Aunt Jillian was a citizen, someone with a house and a good job and a wonderful, perfect life in the land of milk and honey—or at least the land of non-dairy creamer and NutraSweet. Aunt Jillian was the reason I had to do well in school because I had to go to the same prestigious high school and meet all the same targets she had. My mom had not been great at school. But I was supposed to be a top student, like Aunt Jillian, be president of the French club, become a swimming champ, lead the debate team etc etc. I was supposed to be everything my mother had never had the chance to be, and do everything Jillian had done so effortlessly.

And then, all of a sudden, Jillian was *not someone to take pattern from*?

Now, understand that I'd met Jillian once in my life. When I was six, my grandmother died. Jillian came home for the funeral and stayed to visit for three weeks. I will never forget her sweetly fragrant suitcases full of clothes and shoes and presents for my mother and me. The schoolgirl in the faded pictures in my mother's photo album had grown up. I remembered her as a big woman with a short head of hair. Aunt Jillian wasn't married; my mom said loudly to anyone who asked that Jillian wasn't in the market for a man and would never be. The Jillian I met wore lots of shiny, silver jewellery in her ears (from lobe to top), around her neck and on her wrists and her fingers, and even in her nose. She never wore makeup and she was always in jeans and a black T-shirt, no matter what the weather. She said she had worked too hard at everything else to work at style, too. At six years old I accepted the explanation. And as I got older, if I ever gave Jillian a thought, it was, *People can be different, right*?

Of course, when you're a child and your island is the world and your world doesn't include a sophisticated understanding of the world, none of that means anything to you. It was only when I got to Canada and moved into her house that I understood.

Aunt Jillian wasn't single, and she wasn't a fashion victim.

Aunt Jillian was gay.

When you're little there's a lot you take for granted. I never really thought about my mother or her family. My grandfather died before I was born, and my grandmother died of breast cancer when I was just a little kid. Aunt Jillian was not really a part of our day-to-day lives because she lived in Canada and she and my mom weren't all that close. Yeah, we were Facebook friends but I really hadn't paid her that much attention. Was I completely oblivious to the fact that she was obviously, visibly queer? Pretty much. What can I say? It just didn't occur to me at all before I moved to Edmonton.

Sounds strange to say because I am an only child, but I was never my mother's favourite. I felt she had a quiet contempt for everything about me. My hair was just one of the problems, which is actually funny because there's nobody in the world I resemble more than my mother. We're both slender and dark, with the same thick, short hair. I guess I got my height from my dad—my mother doesn't talk about him much and I confess I don't have too much interest in the guy who abandoned us before I was born. *Jerk*.

What's really weird is that all my life my mother had compared me to Jillian. It happened all the time. If I picked up a book that Jillian might have liked, my mother commented on it. When I wanted to go to the convent school mom brought up the fact that it was where Jillian had gone—as if I could forget given the photos I'd seen all my life of Jillian so proud in her convent uniform. (And when I failed the exam—or rather, failed to pass for the convent school, my mother never stopped mentioning it.) My mother seemed to constantly talk about Jillian's accomplishments, her likes and her dislikes, what she used to do as a child, what she used to say, what Jillian used to look like before she cut off her wild, curly hair. Somehow she never mentioned that Jillian was not just gay, but practically married to a woman named Julie.

Chapter
3

I knocked on the back door before I slipped my key into the lock, just being polite as my mother had taught me to be. After all, this wasn't my house, even if it was where I lived at the moment. As usual nobody answered. Jillian and Julie were down in the basement at work.

They ran a little web design company and were trying to branch out into ebook publishing. I didn't know anything about this kind of thing—nobody I knew of published books in Trinidad. I wondered if it was the same as publishing your stories online. You could find some decent stories on the Internet, like one I had read one day at the library about a girl who fell in love with her neighbour and tried to kill herself when their parents broke them up. I liked the writing, but I couldn't believe the girl actually told her mother she was going to attempt suicide. I never told any adults that I was sad all the time and that I wanted to kill myself. They only really paid attention after I swallowed a bottle of pills and started vomiting blood on my mother's kitchen floor.

The web design stuff Aunt Jillian and Julie did was mad decent, though quite frankly I don't care about how the Internet actually works, only that it does. I had email and stuff, and a Facebook account—the usual—but when I had my *troubles*, as my mother calls my suicide attempt, I deleted all my accounts. I haven't turned anything back on yet except my Skype. Maybe I never will. The other day I read some magazine articles about how having smartphones makes kids depressed. Maybe that's true, but I know I had the hole in my belly long before I knew what a smartphone was. It wasn't seeing posts about my friends having a good time that made me sick; I had no friends in the first place. I'm a Caribbean hermit in exile in Edmonton. Talking to Akilah was my one lifeline.

I went into the house. This kitchen floor, like everything else in Jillian and Julie's house, was spotless. Julie was a fiend for cleaning. Saturdays she'd attack dirt like she had a personal vendetta against it. She would maintain a low-grade surveillance on it and there would be occasional sniper fire at it for the rest of the week. My mom was a good housekeeper but next to Julie she seemed slovenly. There was dust on our bookshelves! Not here. Julie even took a cloth and wiped the books themselves. The kitchen was her special domain, and it always smelled a little of pine cleaner. I've never seen a breadcrumb or juice stain on the kitchen counters, and a glass didn't get the chance to sit in the sink for more than a minute or two before Julie swept in to wash up. That was the case this afternoon. From the bottle they always kept in the fridge I poured myself a glass of cranberry juice and then put the glass in the sink. I went to my room to put down my backpack and the books I had borrowed at the library and by the time I came back the glass was washed and turned down on the drip tray. There was no sign of Julie herself, though.

"Julie!" I yelled down the stairs, standing at the top. "I would have washed it, you know!"

"I know, sweetie!" she yelled back. In a second I heard Aunt Jillian's heavy footsteps on the wooden stairs.

"Hey, muffin," she said, as her short curly Afro popped into view. "What's up?"

"Oh, nothing much. A cop tried to pick me up at the bus stop," I said. "I told him I was fourteen and he backed off in a hurry."

Unlike my mother, who made me feel bad for feeling sad, Jillian and Julie acted like I was normal. It was an unusual feeling, being thought of as normal, but a good one. It made me feel almost happy.

"Did you tell him that your aunt would kill him too?" Jillian asked, drily.

"Oh, no, we didn't get that well-acquainted."

"Really," she said, pouring herself some juice. "What did you do today? Go to the gym?" She peered at my sneakers, which were starting to look a hot mess. The lacings—let's say they used to be white; and the soles were decidedly un-perky. I didn't go to the gym every day but, combined with all the walking I did, it was enough to take its toll on my footwear.

"Nah," I said, scuffing my toe in embarrassment. Jillian had to be paying for this visit because my mom didn't make that much money. I didn't want Jillian to feel I was taking advantage of her generosity. She was always getting me stuff, little things like music on iTunes and cute notebooks and pens and T-shirts, and I couldn't say no. A pair of sneakers would be just one more thing she got me but I didn't want to be the one to ask for them.

"Looks like we need to take you to the mall for some trainers," she surmised, seeing past my gestures.

"Yeah, maybe."

"We were going to go out to dinner anyway, maybe we could stop on the way there. Guess what!"

"What?"

"We got our first contract to publish an ebook!"

"Yay, I think?" As I said, I didn't really know anything about publishing books, electronic or otherwise.

"Yay, definitely," she confirmed. "It's just one but it's a start. A writer in California saw our ad on an LGBT publishing Facebook page and she messaged us this afternoon. She said she was glad to give her business to a fellow lesbian."

I squirmed a little bit when she said "lesbian". I had been living with her and Julie for a couple of months and obviously I knew that they were gay but it wasn't something I was comfortable talking about with them. They were amused and sometimes exasperated by my attitude but didn't let it change the way they behaved, either towards each other or towards me. I did know that LGBT meant "lesbian, gay, bisexual and transgender," which, if you think about it, is a bunch of very different kinds of people, but still people who think they have more in common with each other than they have with the straight world.

I'm straight. At least, I think I'm straight. I have never tested the hypothesis, never having had a boyfriend, but I figure I've never wanted to have a girlfriend, either. Or to be somebody else's boyfriend, come to think of it. I've heard of women who have operations to become men and get married to women as men and stuff like that. That's pretty weird to me. I mean, you're born one thing and you should stay that thing, that's what I feel. But I guess I don't know what it's like to be trapped inside the wrong body, which is how some of these people feel. Or maybe I do, in a way. Maybe I'm in the wrong body and that's why I am so sad all the time.

I've never talked to Aunt Jillian about what it's like to be a lesbian. Maybe I will, one day. But for now, it's okay for us to just sip cranberry juice in the kitchen and look at the bright afternoon outside the window.

Julie came upstairs and gave me a belly noogie through my T-shirt.

My T-shirt was white with a frog on it. The frog was wearing a crown and had a speech bubble that said, "Any day now, princess." It's really a guy's T-shirt but I thought it was so funny that they bought it for me at the ginormous mall that was my first tourist stop in Edmonton. Guy stuff and girl stuff don't mean that much to me, mostly. It's too stressful to think about it. I'm not really into the clothes and look of an average teenage girl, anyway; especially since I cut off all my hair, I just wear whatever I want to. Needless to say, that just pisses my mother off even more.

"Why don't you at least try to *look* normal?" my mother used to ask me.

There really isn't an answer to that is there.

Jillian told Julie she wanted to get me some new shoes at the mall and Julie nodded, wiping imaginary dirt from the kitchen counters. "For dinner: Mexican or Italian?" Jillian asked her.

"Oh, I don't know. What do you think, kid?"

As usual I had no idea. Mexican was nice. But Italian was nice, too. And, come to think of it, so was steak, the other option that they didn't mention but which nevertheless was always available. They both loved red meat, despite what the doctors kept saying on TV about how it was full of cholesterol and hormones and was really, really bad for you. They ate steak a couple of times a week and they seemed pretty healthy, I thought. But then again, they weren't really that old, only in their thirties. Julie was a little bit older than Jillian, not that she looked it.

Julie looked like a pixie, tiny and pretty, with bright black eyes. She wore lots of jeans and T-shirts, too, like Jillian, but sometimes she varied it with traditional Indian clothes like saris and *khurtas*, a kind of long-sleeved man's tunic with buttons at the neck and slits

24

up the sides. She had about a dozen of them in different colours, and she wore them in place of a business suit when she had anything official or important to do. She wore saris to really dress up. When she dressed up, Julie looked like an Indian film star, like Preeti Jhangiani or one of them from the movies she liked to watch. On the other hand, Jillian's idea of dressing up was to wear a blazer over her T-shirt and jeans.

Julie's hair was long and straight, way past her waist. She kept saying it was a pain in the butt but she wouldn't cut it for the world. Now she swept it up into a bun as she walked out of the kitchen. "You gals make up your minds and I'll be in the shower while you do it."

It was going on six in the evening, but there were still a good three hours of daylight left. *Home home* was different. In the Caribbean, the sun comes up around six every morning, all year long, and goes down around six every evening, all year long. Sometimes the sun comes up at five and goes down at six-thirty at night. But those are the extremes. Here, in Canada, the sun could come up at six and go down at nine at night, or come up at eight and go down at three in the afternoon. It was, to me, entirely magical and a bit astounding. I would have to be there for years before I got used to eating dinner in the daylight.

"Thinking about doing a barbecue next Saturday," Jillian said. "What you think?"

I grunted. If she had a barbecue it would mean about twenty people in and out of the house over the course of two days, since guests would come on Saturday and a few would not leave until late Sunday. I had been through two of her barbecues before and knew what to expect. It wasn't bad but some of the people tried to talk to me—and that was just too scary. I came out of my room to eat and to use the bathroom and to show my face, just to be polite, but that was about it. I couldn't do socialising. Socialising made me feel the big, yawning hole in my belly worse than ever, a feeling that no pill could ever entirely control.

I didn't tell Jillian that but she must have guessed something like it because she didn't pressure me to come out and be social. She and Julie still entertained but had cut down considerably, one because they had an extra mouth to feed and it was cutting into their entertainment budget, and two because they knew it made me feel uncomfortable. It was hard for them to ignore how withdrawn and uncomfortable I became when they had company.

I heard the shower in Jillian and Julie's room start up and I pushed myself off the kitchen counter, heading to the other bathroom to start my own preparations for going to the mall and then dinner. I had about an hour to decide what to wear. I would need every second of it.

I was peering into the closet trying to decide which of my outfits would be the least offensive to wear when the burbling ringtone started up on my phone. It was Akilah again. She was out of her church clothes and back at home. I recognised her bedroom in the background.

"You survived?"

"Yeah, thanks," I said with a sigh. I sat on the bed while we talked. "Sorry to be such a pain."

"You're not a pain. That's what friends are for," she said.

"Ki-ki, what should I wear?" I groaned in frustration.

"Since when do you care what you wear?" she answered, chuckling. We both knew I was rather offhand about my appearance.

"We're going out to dinner," I said with a moan. "All I ever wear is jeans and T-shirts. I just feel like my aunt would appreciate me wearing something different for a change."

"I haven't seen you in a dress since our Fifth Standard Christmas bazaar," Akilah teased. "Besides, you look good in jeans and T-shirt. Make that booty pop," she said. I looked at her wide grin on the screen, trying to decide whether she was being serious or not.

"Leave my booty out of it," I murmured.

"What kind of Trinidadian woman are you, if you don't care about your bottom?" Now she was laughing outright. "We sing songs about it, even! '*Sugar Bum, Sugar Bum-Bum*'," she sang.

The lyrics to a famous calypso didn't impress me. "Blah blah blah," I answered. "Ki-ki? Do you think I'm pretty?"

She was quiet for a long moment. "Yeah, sometimes."

"Wow, that's a really ringing endorsement."

"No, that's not what I mean," she said. "You have a really pretty face and a nice figure but you hide yourself away in baggy, shapeless clothes like you're afraid someone will notice you're pretty. That's why I said 'sometimes'. What I should have said is you're always pretty but sometimes you don't let it show. It's like you're scared of people finding you attractive."

"Meh, shut up." I scowled but I knew she was right. I had major hang-ups about the way I looked. "You know that every Trinidadian boy only wants a red-skinned girlfriend with long, curly hair and a big bottom. Brown-skinned girls are okay, but their lips and noses can't be too African—"

"Boys are dumb and you know that."

"Yeah but I'm too dark, my hair is too picky, and worst of all my bottom is flat! I'll never get a boyfriend," I bawled in mock agony.

"Papa! I never knew you wanted a boyfriend," Akilah teased. "You always have your head stuck in a book. Boys at your school don't even know you exist."

"How would you know about my school, anyway?" I grumbled. It killed me that Akilah—who always aced *her* exams—had been placed in the very convent school I had dreamed of attending, while I had been placed in a government secondary school. All because of one exam. Most of the population thought her school was far superior to mine. And, by extension, its students were thought of as far superior. But that was neither here nor there in this conversation. The point was that she went to an all-girls' school, so how would she know what boys at my co-ed school thought of me?

"I saw that girl we went to primary school with—what's her name? Britney?—at the mall. You might think nobody talks your business but she said your whole school is full of rumours about why you left so suddenly in the middle of the school year. Everyone is saying that you got pregnant and your mother sent you away—except that nobody can work out who you could be pregnant for. Most of them think that you have never been alone with a boy in your life."

"Immaculate conception, then?" I giggled. I was not at all religious. And "they", whoever they were, were right. I had never been alone with a boy in my life. To be honest I wouldn't know what to do if a boy found me interesting. And the thought that anybody was talking about me made me a little sick. I much preferred to be invisible. But I put those thoughts behind me. "Ki-ki, back to me and my problems. What am I going to wear?"

Chapter

4

We walked into the restaurant—Mexican, after all—and I nearly died in my brand-new sneakers.

This boy who was sitting down at one of the tables with these two good-looking, oldish white guys, was the most gorgeous guy I'd ever seen. He was about sixteen, with clear skin the colour of an apple about ten minutes after it's been cut, sort of caramely brown but not so buttery. He had curly hair so perfect that it looked like an advertisement for curly hair. He had hazel eyes and long eyelashes and pink lips and a button nose and reddish-brown freckles on his high cheekbones. I had never seen anybody so good looking in real life before. I mean, I'd seen movie stars on screen and they were good-looking, but Tom Cruise is really only about half my height in real life so I figured there were lots of things that clever camera angles could simulate, including good looks.

There were no clever camera angles here. Just the best-looking guy I'd ever seen. He was also tall AF, judging by the length of the legs I saw folded under the table and the length of the arms I saw folded above it.

And then Julie and Aunt Jillian caused me to have a minor heart attack in the middle of the restaurant.

"It's Nathan and Bill!" said Julie to Jillian.

"Wow, I haven't seen them in ages! I wonder if they've ordered yet."

We ended up sitting at their table and having dinner together, me next to the most gorgeous boy I'd ever seen in real life. I wished I could call Akilah instantly to discuss the new development and the terror I felt, but I knew if I pulled out my phone it would be rude and Jillian and Julie would be disappointed in me. So I sat at the table, ducked my head and tried not to pass out from lack of oxygen.

I should have said steak. It's less messy than Mexican, which is all sauce and burritos and dips and has all kinds of potential for falling on the clothes that I obviously shouldn't have worn. They were cool for the mall but now there was this guy and we were at dinner and I felt I looked like a slob in skinny jeans and a flannel shirt. And those new sneakers were so obnoxiously shiny. My mouth was dry and ashy. I should have at least put on some Chap Stick. I felt horribly unprepared for the moment. There was a sick feeling in the pit of my stomach. Imagining the way I must have seemed to the cute boy, I was filled with self-disgust. I couldn't eat.

Jillian looked at me from time to time while she chatted with Nathan and his partner Bill. They were old friends of hers, two lawyers she had met at college and who had, like her, stayed in Edmonton after graduation. The gorgeous kid was Nathan's son, born of his former marriage.

"Nathan used to run after me back in the days when he thought I was straight," Jillian confided to me in an outrageously loud whisper, much to the kid's mortification and the other adults' amusement. *Good*, I thought, watching the cute boy blush in embarrassment. *At least I'm not the only one who has to suffer through this ordeal.*

The kid's name was Joshua. He lived with his mom in the States but was visiting his dad for the summer. Biracial kids like Joshua had a hard time living in largely white communities like Edmonton, Nathan said. I nodded, choking down a piece of chicken. I personally thought Edmonton was as homogenous as you wanted it to be. I saw plenty of black and brown people in the city. Even at that table, there was diversity: Julie was born in Canada but she was Indian (she called herself "South Asian") and Jillian was black, from Trinidad, and they were gay, a minority in itself—but Nathan didn't seem to think they counted towards the diversity of the community.

He and Bill were work partners, not romantic partners. They had a practice downtown but for some reason they hadn't hung out with Jillian and Julie for a really long time. As Nathan kept talking, I began to guess why. When he talked, he called native Canadians and the poor "those people". I wondered what he called black people when his son and other black people weren't around. Having the world at your feet can do that to you, I guess. Joshua just sat there with his face turning redder and redder; soon he was the same colour as his freckles.

I didn't say much. I toyed with my phone, spinning it around and around on the table.

Joshua and I kept sneaking glances at each other when we thought the other wasn't looking, a fact that wasn't lost on Nathan, who thought it was a good idea to draw attention to our furtive looks. I thought the restaurant floor should open right up and let me in but it didn't and I was stuck there, sitting next to this gorgeous boy and feeling sicker and sicker.

As soon as I could I excused myself and ran away to the bathroom. I leaned against the big mirror. It was surrounded by tiny sombreros and maracas and chilli peppers. It was super cheesy, but it didn't matter to me. All I felt was my deep shame, and the awful pain in the centre of my belly. I took about ten deep breaths. *I will not scream, I will not scream, I will not scream.*

Somebody was trying to come in, pushing against the door, so I went into one of the three cubicles to hide. Locked in, I went through the mantra again. *I will not scream, I will not scream, I will not scream.*

I reached a shaky hand into my pocket for my phone, but it wasn't there. I must have left it on the table when I fled.

I will not scream, I will not scream.

Nope.

I screamed. I stuffed my fist in my mouth and I screamed and screamed again. It was a little scream, though. And I quickly got my act together and stopped crying and stopped my hands from shaking and generally tried to sound normal when the woman in the stall next to mine asked very timidly, "Are you okay in there?"

"Oh, fine, fine," I said. "Just letting off a little steam." I closed my eyes and felt my sense of hopelessness rising higher and higher. At first I desperately wanted my phone so I could call Akilah, but then as my dread worsened I thought I'd already burdened her with one stupid panic attack so I shouldn't bother her again with another so soon.

The woman left the bathroom and I stayed in there for another few minutes. I put the seat cover down and sat on it, rocking back and forth and squeezing my eyes shut to try to not feel so bad but nothing was working. My pounding heart felt like it wanted to jump out of my mouth. Eventually, Julie came in.

"You alright in there, muffin?"

I didn't answer. I couldn't. If I'd tried I'd have started bawling really hard.

"Honey?" She sounded worried. "Open the door. Let me in."

I let her in. She took a look at me and hugged me tight and said it'd be okay. That didn't help much, only made me want to cry more, and so I did cry more. I also started hitting my balled fists against my thighs.

I'm on some pretty strong antidepressants and anti-anxiety meds, and I have been since they sent me to the hospital after my attempt. A group of doctors, quiet as a cloud, drifted from bed to bed in the children's ward where I had been sent. A kind-faced male doctor seemed to do the talking for the team as he explained my wonky brain chemistry, and said that I might have to take meds for the rest of my life. *Nice.*

Anyway, the medication isn't the only thing they prescribed. I'm also supposed to be in talk therapy, but my mom couldn't afford it in Trinidad and I had rejected any suggestion of it in Edmonton when I had started seeing Dr Khan, my doctor here. Every now and then my aunt gently raised the question but I always changed the subject. I was taking my meds—antidepressant in the morning, anti-anxietal at night. That was all I could do for now and since I had been in Edmonton it had worked to keep me more or less okay. I had felt panic sometimes, but I didn't generally want to tear my own face off; I felt sadness, but not the giant abyss that I had wanted to fall into the day I took the bottle of pills, to fall and never return.

But those good old days of managing my depression and anxiety with just medication seemed to be over. I was having a grand mal meltdown in the bathroom of Tacos and Tequila.

After holding me for a few minutes, Julie sat me down, told me not to worry and left to fetch Aunt Jillian.

When my aunt came, she went into crisis mode. "Right. Let's get her out of here and back home. We'll deal with this better there."

Though I was kind of glad I didn't have to see the obscenely cute boy again, somewhere under the weeping, wailing and gnashing of teeth I was a bit sorry. He really was cute. That was the last coherent thought I had for a long time.

Chapter

5

I cried all night. Then I stopped crying for a while but I wouldn't eat anything. And then I ate some crackers but I wouldn't talk. It felt as though I didn't sleep at all. I wallowed in my self-loathing and my terror of the world outside of my bed. There was nothing I could do but feel pitiful and hate everything about myself—and hate myself even more for feeling the way I did. Every few hours I heard that bubbling, babbling ringtone —it was Akilah, but I just couldn't face answering it. Just the thought of talking to anybody made me cry again even harder.

At the end of the second day, Jillian brought Dr Khan to see me. He tried talking to me, asking what had triggered the panic attack, but I turned my back and stared at the wall. Eventually he left and told my aunt he'd come back the next day. I had a feeling I could no longer convince him I'd be fine with just my meds, as I had when I'd seen him last month.

Akilah called again. I picked up this time.

"Oh my God, I've been so worried! Are you okay?" Akilah's panic showed on her face and in her voice. She was frantic. "You didn't go and do anything to hurt yourself—?"

I groaned. Tears trembled in my eyes. "I'm alive. But I can't talk, okay? I'm sorry." And I hung up on my very best and only friend. Which made me feel so bad I started to panic again. *What was wrong with me? Why couldn't I just be normal?*

Tears, snot, anguish. Lather, rinse, repeat.

Dr Khan gave Aunt Jillian some sleeping pills (for me, not for her, though I can't imagine she was getting much rest, between my caterwauling and the sheer worry she must have felt) and told her to keep an eye on me. Since I'd already proven that I was capable of taking an overdose, Jillian kept my meds and doled them out to me as prescribed. The new sleeping pills knocked me out for hours at a time. From what I remember, I didn't think about anything much in between bouts of sleep. I mostly lay around feeling wretched, feeling a deep, inner agony that I couldn't touch or see but which was nonetheless like a gaping wound somewhere inside of me. I did want to die; that I remember. Death was the only thing I felt would stop the pain of my existence. Like turning out a light. Snap. Done.

Julie and Jillian took turns sitting with me practically around the clock. I would fall asleep with my head in Julie's lap and wake up in Jillian's arms, hardly knowing one hour from another.

The next day Dr Khan came back, asking again what had triggered the panic attack.

"Was it… because of the boy?" Julie nervously prompted.

This whole episode wasn't really anything to do with Joshua or his dad. Yes, it was the awfully uncomfortable dinner that proved the tipping point, but honestly it could have been anything pushing me over the edge. I had known since earlier in the week that something was up. I knew I was feeling sadder and more hopeless and scared than I had been since coming to Edmonton, and the awkward dinner somehow, in my tangled reasoning, seemed to be all my fault.

Dr Khan smiled at me hopefully, waiting for me to say some of those things out loud. At first I couldn't.

Gradually we started talking, me mostly just answering questions in monosyllables. Though I had been under Dr Khan's care since I had been in Edmonton, he had never seen me crash before. He asked lots of questions I recognised from talks I'd had with my hospital shrinks in Trinidad—about how I felt and what usually made me feel this way. I kept glancing over at Jillian and Julie. My mother had responded very coldly to this part of my treatment, making me feel as though my whole life was inadequate and that I was only making things harder for her as a single mom. But Jillian and Julie didn't. They held hands and looked worried while the doctor asked the first few questions, and eventually they ducked out of the room to give us some privacy.

"Antidepressants don't work overnight," Dr Khan said, telling me what I already knew. "They take weeks to be absorbed into your system."

In my case, he explained, the medication I had been on since my *troubles* began took about three weeks to take effect, and as long as two months to really work. He asked if I felt the meds had been helping.

"Kinda. They help me not feel so sad. Sometimes." Sometimes I still felt like I had the Grand Canyon in my belly, but to be honest those times had been getting further and further apart.

"All your walking, swimming and going to the gym also help," he said.

"The doctors at the hospital at home—well, *home home*"—I said with a frightened glance at the door, in case I had overstepped by calling my aunt's house "home"—"they told me to get plenty of exercise and sunshine and to take my medication religiously."

"Yup," Dr Khan said. "Depression and its close buddy anxiety are mental illnesses, but they have physical aspects as well, and most people don't realise how much exercise can help."

Since my *troubles* began I'd been doing a lot of reading on depression and anxiety. For example, I knew that plenty of teens and even some little kids suffer with depression, even though adults are like, "What do *you* have to be depressed about?" I know that part of the cause of my problem is my brain chemistry. People who have depression don't make enough of this brain chemical called serotonin, which scientists think helps make you happy. The most popular kind of antidepressant helps your brain build up more serotonin so you feel happier. But your brain also makes serotonin (and other feel-good chemicals) when you exercise, and when you're hugged, and from sunshine. I couldn't honestly say if I had been feeling better because of the medication or because I was getting so much exercise, walking and swimming in that weak Canadian sunshine, and getting plenty of hugs from Jillian and Julie. And anyway, for the past few days the paralysing pain and self-hatred had come back as strong as ever.

Most adults don't believe children can get anxiety, but believe me, we do. My anxiety kept me up at night. I would worry about failing at school, every stupid thing I said to other people, global warming, my mother, the father I never knew. Fear would sometimes keep me up at night, gnawing at my guts and closing up my throat. Akilah told me that I worried for nothing, but her words meant little to me and certainly didn't help me sleep when I was staring up at the ceiling in the dark of the night. When they first gave me the medication for my anxiety it made me doze, which was great for my sleeplessness. As the weeks went on, though, it was less and less effective. This meant my nightly vigil over all the bad things, real or imagined, had started up again about two weeks before what we shall now refer to as *The Tacos and Tequila Incident.*

The doctor and I talked for about forty-five minutes and then he talked to Julie and Jillian alone for another ten minutes about what to expect in the next few days: I'd be very quiet, probably, and would take some time to get back on my feet. He told them not to push me too much, but not to baby me either. I was sick but not physically helpless. And they should encourage me to get out of bed and out of the house, though I probably should not be on my own for a little while.

Dr Khan scheduled a talk therapy session that would take place two days later. I tried to resist but both he and Jillian gave me such stern looks that my protestations crumpled. I guess I would have to try talk therapy after all.

When he left, Jillian walked him out. I was alone with Julie, coherent and normal for the first time in days. I felt so embarrassed about the way I had cried, the way I had felt.

"I'm really sorry about this," I muttered to her.

"Oh, muffin," she said. "Don't worry about it. We knew what to expect when we asked you to stay with us."

"Yeah. But it's so...." I didn't know what to say. I felt ashamed of how I had behaved, even though I knew that I really didn't have any choice about it. Clinical depression and panic disorders have minds of their own.

"Hey. Don't worry about it," said Julie, with a firmness I seldom heard in her sweetly musical voice. "What do you want for dinner?"

I shrugged. Like I said before, making decisions was one of the hardest things for me. Even simple things like what to wear and what to eat for lunch overwhelmed me sometimes.

"Curry?"

"Uh. Yeah," I said. Julie's chicken curry was amazing. And she made it with basmati rice and about six different side vegetables, each served in a little silver bowl. My favourite was dhal, yellow split peas made into a puree. All that cooking should have taken hours but Julie somehow did it in two twos. When Jillian came back into the bedroom Julie slipped out to start dinner. In moments I smelled the wonderful aromas of frying garlic and *geera*. They called *geera* cumin in Canada.

Jillian was looking at me with a little half-smile.

"Chickie! You had us really scared for a while."

"Yeah, I'm sorry," I repeated. "I'm too much trouble."

"Nonsense! We love you. And we knew you were sick when we invited you to stay with us," she said, echoing what Julie had said. I think they had worked out a spiel in advance.

"Want to go outside?"

I shook my head. I had no idea what day it was or what time it was but I knew that it had been quite some time since my last bath. I felt sticky and dirty and could feel a layer of grit on my teeth. "Think I'll take a shower."

She smiled encouragingly, helped me up and led me to the bathroom. She sat on the edge of the bathtub while I brushed my teeth then moved to lean against the sink while I had my shower.

My back hurt from lying in bed so long. My hands were shaking.

I pulled on some clean clothes and sat on the edge of my bed for a while next to Jillian, both of us silent. By then the house was full of the pungent smell of curry and the aromatic scent of basmati rice.

I suddenly realised that my last real meal had been the half-eaten chicken at Tacos and Tequila. Remembering that reminded me that I had had my freak-out session in the presence of a gorgeous boy, the most gorgeous boy I had ever seen in my entire life. I groaned and hid my face in a pillow. Jillian put her hand on my shoulder and rubbed it lightly, no doubt gearing up to deal with another meltdown.

"Don't worry," I said, my voice muffled by the pillow, "I'm not going to trip off. I was just remembering how I messed up in front of—"

I gulped my last words down. "What?" Jillian asked.

"Nothing."

I got up and we went outside to the deck. The tubs of summer flowers in the back yard seemed way too bright after my seeing nothing but blank walls and bed linen for days. There was a light breeze blowing. The flowers bobbed their heads in the rustic-looking planters. A few leaves blew off the neighbour's maple tree, falling on the neat, green lawn. I picked up a rake and went to gather the stray leaves. When I'd raked them into a little pile, Jillian and I sat on the patio chairs and just looked out at the dancing flowers. My hands were still shaking.

In a while, Julie came out to join us. "Dinner's almost done," she said, wiping her hands on a paper towel. Dropping an absent-minded kiss on the top of Jillian's head, she took a seat next to us. "What do you want to do tomorrow?" she asked me.

"Dunno," I said.

"Swimming or gym?" Jillian said, mindful of the doctor's words about exercise.

"Swimming, I guess," I said, after a minute. Then I felt guilty about the new sneakers and said instead, "No; gym."

"We should take turns taking her around," Julie suggested to Jillian. "I'll take her tomorrow, you could do the next day."

"Don't you think I should take her out first?" Jillian responded.

"Um, hello?" I said. "I am sitting right here." Julie looked abashed, but only a little bit. "Besides, it doesn't matter. I'll be okay with either one of you."

Julie beamed at me. I didn't say it out loud but what I meant was that she was equally as important to me as Jillian—who looked at me with a big grin when she caught on.

"Well, look at us," Jillian said. "One big happy."

Maybe not *happy*, not yet. But one big something, for sure.

Chapter

6

My mom called regularly. That was a good thing and a bad thing. I know it might not sound like it, but I love my mom. She gave me life and I owe her my good cheekbones and my long legs and my razor-sharp wit and my love of reading. But I've always been a huge disappointment to her. I look into her eyes and see the shadowed hopes that one day I'll turn into the kind of girl she wanted: a nice, sweet, kind girl who wears frocks, goes to parties, has lots of friends, goes to a good school and does well in all the suitable subjects. What she ended up with was me. I knew that every time she looked at me she saw all the things I could have been but—as she puts it—I chose not to be. I was a walking disappointment to her.

And that was before I tried to OD.

Because I'm an only child, there's not even a sibling to take the pressure off me. My mom had Aunt Jillian to compare herself to all her life—and that must have been terrible, since Jillian was pretty much perfect, except for the teeny, tiny fact that she was a homosexual. Worse yet, my mom was the cheap, knockoff version of Jillian. Younger by two years, she was not as pretty, not as smart, and not as ambitious. Jillian left Trinidad at seventeen to study in Canada and never moved back *home home*. By Canadian standards she wasn't a great success, just average, but by island standards anything one does "Away" is made that much more special and exciting and extraordinary. My mom on the other hand became a primary school clerk, went to work at eight in the morning and got home at five in

42

the afternoon. It was a job she could do while taking care of me, not a vocation. She had a comfortable, boring life—nothing like Jillian's. As a magazine writer Jillian was always jetting around Canada and the US for stories, getting to meet lots and lots of people.

Jillian didn't tell my mom that she had to struggle in between all that jetting around because she didn't have a steady job and she lived hand to mouth. She had no savings, no insurance and no backup plan for her retirement. Jillian told me, in one of our first conversations when I got to Canada, that she envied my mom's stability. Jillian wished she had a family and a pension. "Oi vey!" she said with a laugh. "I'd do anything to know that when I'm sixty I can sit back if I want to."

One of the reasons she and Julie had set up the publishing company was so that they could get more stability. And Jillian had given up her magazine work.

One night when I was going to the bathroom really late I overheard Jillian and her girlfriend having an argument about babies. Jillian wanted one and Julie didn't. I didn't see how two women could be mothers to one child, without a father, but it seemed that Jillian could. She was telling Julie that she really wished she could be a mother and that she was jealous of my mom because she had me.

I guess up until that point I had never considered myself such a prize. Imagine that someone wanted me! *Me!* I never talked to my aunt about it, because I didn't want her to know I had listened to their private conversation, but it stuck in my mind. It was the first time I realised that someone *wanted* me in their life.

My mother certainly never behaved like that. She didn't ill-treat me. She was a decent mother and not abusive or anything. I got the normal one or two slaps for bad behaviour most Caribbean kids got from their mothers. Yet neither by word nor deed did she show she really wanted me around. She did what she had to do. I was a chore, a responsibility, but not a pleasure and definitely not a privilege.

Now that I was in exile, every week, like clockwork, my mom would phone or Skype me. She'd ask the same questions, carefully avoiding any mention of my illness. We didn't talk about it anymore, after her first recriminations and attempts to blame me for my craziness. Now she pretended I was on holiday. My *troubles* had somehow turned into an extended vaycay.

She called on the phone this time. After a two-minute chat—one-sided, she did most of the talking—I handed the phone over to Jillian.

"Cynthia! How are you?"

Jillian was always nice on the phone with my mom. She was her sister, after all.

"Oh, things are going well…" She told mom about her new contract, leaving out the LGBT connection. My family was full of *things best left unsaid*.

"Oh, she's doing great." She threw me a look. "Cynthia, I don't want you to panic but she had a little setback.

"Small.

"Four days.

"No, she didn't.

"But—

"Yes.

"Cynthia, lis—

"Cynthia! Listen to me. She's fine. No, you don't need to come. She's doing much better now. It was last week and the doctor has seen her. She's doing fine now," she repeated.

At that point I drifted back to my room. I had heard all I wanted to hear. Obviously my mother was going to try to convince Jillian to send me back to Trinidad. I hoped Jillian would stand up to her.

I was lying on my back, staring up at the plain white ceiling, when my aunt came in.

"Well that was hard," she announced. I didn't reply. "Hey, sport." She held my chin and turned my head to look at her.

"Am I going back?" It was all I wanted to know.

She looked surprised. "No! I told her you were fine, didn't you hear me?"

I snorted. "As if she listens to anybody."

"She listens to me. I'm her big sister, you know! I told her you were in good hands. Am I right or am I right?"

Reluctantly I smiled. "You're right."

"Scooch over," she said, lying on the bed next to me and taking my icy hand.

"Cold hands, warm heart," she intoned, a relic from her childhood that I too knew from my own. In a lot of ways, things hadn't changed in the Caribbean since she was a girl. "Baby, you're going to stay here until you're ready to go home. Don't worry about your mom, okay? I'll handle her."

Little tears started slipping from the corners of my eyes. "I'll never want to go back home."

"Sure you will, one day. But right now you can just stay here until you feel ready. Don't worry. You'll be my little girl until then. And this can be your home."

I buried my head in her shoulder and cried.

After a while my sobbing stopped. I wiped my face with the back of my hand and just lay there smelling her spicy, warm perfume. I sniffed. "What's that you're wearing?"

"Patchouli. It's an herbal perfume. Very hippie-dippy," she said, winking and grinning.

"Are you a hippie?"

The grin stretched further. "Nah, just a good environmentalist. Nobody does animal testing for patchouli," she explained. "Like any good lesbian I have to believe in a cause."

The way she said it was funny but I could tell she was partly serious.

"What does that mean?"

"Well," she said, resting her cheek on my head, "lots of gay people identify with causes—animal rights, the environment, homeless people, immigrant rights, the poor." She thought about it for a second. "I guess, because we know what it's like to be in the minority and the underclass. We know what it's like to have no voice so we try to speak for those who don't either."

I digested that for a while. "What's it like?"

"Patchouli?" she asked, pretending to be serious. "Okay, okay," she giggled as I pinched her arm. "What do you want to know?"

"Well... what's it like being. You know. Gay."

"I don't know what it's like being anything else, so that's a really hard question for me to answer. It's just normal for me. What's it like being straight?"

I shrugged. "I dunno. Normal, I guess."

"See what I mean? But I do feel sometimes—not so much anymore, but I used to feel like I wished I were like you and like Cynthia. I do want babies and a 'normal' life. So it's kind of weird not having those things, but I couldn't really imagine myself any other way."

"Did you ever have a boyfriend?"

"Yup. Did you forget I told you Nathan and I dated? Way before I knew for sure I was gay. We stayed friends, though. His son is my godchild. I wish I saw more of him. Sweet kid. Josh, I mean, not Nate. Nate's a pain in the—"

We laughed at the same time. I was glad she shared my opinion of Nathan. He was arrogant and self-centred. I didn't like him one bit.

"Was he always like that?"

"A jerk?"

I nodded.

"Uh huh. He grew up very privileged and I suppose he never had to think about other people. He likes *exotics* because they give him a glimpse into the other side but—" she shook her head. "Why am I having this conversation with a fourteen-year-old?"

"Cause I asked?"

We laughed again.

"Are you an *exotic*?"

"Yup. So are you. You'll meet lots of people here who think that you're some kind of collector's item just because you have a Caribbean accent and dark skin."

I already had. I thought about the young policeman who tried to talk to me at the bus stop, and others I had met at the library and the gym. "They're always surprised that I talk English and wear normal clothes and stuff," I said. Then I thought about Julie's version of "normal", the Indian clothes she called "Desi high fashion", and reconsidered my language. "Western clothes, I mean."

"Right. Not everybody's like that but some people are. Nathan married a Jamaican, that's Josh's mom, and I think Nate was always surprised that she was brighter and better educated than he was."

I chuckled.

"But Josh seems like a good kid," she repeated. "What do you think about him?"

I blushed and bit my bottom lip. If the earth had opened up right at that moment it would have been awesome.

"Ooh! Looks like somebody has a crush!"

"Aunty!"

"Oh, alright. I'll stop teasing. I have to give you fair warning, though: I'm inviting them over to the barbecue."

"Barbecue!" I said in dismay. "What barbecue?"

Next weekend, it turned out. They were taking the doctor's advice and taking life back to its ordinary level. I didn't have to participate, but my aunt told me I'd be expected to come out and say hello at least.

Hesitantly, I agreed. "But don't tease me, okay? It makes me feel bad."

"Agreed," she said. No teasing but I had to get ready to talk to the most gorgeous boy I had ever seen, in my temporary home. This time, I hoped, I could do it without having a complete collapse.

I called Akilah as soon as Jillian closed the door.

"Ki-ki!" I wailed.

"What? Are you okay?" She had obviously prepared herself for the worst. It had been ages since I had talked to her. She looked scared, her eyes open wide and her mouth trembling. "I was so worried!"

I calmed her down and told her about the awful past few days, the sleeping pills that knocked me out, Dr Khan and his advice to exercise and his threat—um, I mean *promise*—that we would continue talk therapy soon.

"Why are you hating on therapy so much?" Akilah asked. She sat at her kitchen table. Her mom was cutting up vegetables in the background; I heard the rapid whack of a blade on a chopping board and could imagine the kitchen redolent with pungent *chadon beni*, a dark green leafy weed we use for seasoning food in Trinidad. A wave of homesickness hit me. There were so many things I wanted to say but didn't want Aunty Patsy hearing them. And top of the list was the gorgeous kid Josh. Gesticulating to Akilah that she should leave the kitchen had no effect. I typed in the message bar, "GO TO YR ROOM!!! WE HAVE TO TALK!!!!"

Chapter

7

The morning of the barbecue was crisp and clear. Julie was up early, mixing meat, mushrooms and onions into a slurry that she assured me would turn out into the most delicious hamburgers I'd ever tasted. Jillian was out buying charcoal and paper cups and I was assigned to rake the lawn, clean the bathrooms and put out fresh towels. I also had to change the sheets on the pullout sofa bed; people often stayed over after Jillian and Julie's parties.

It was about ten in the morning when I finished my chores and gave a thought to the fact that I had absolutely nothing to wear.

Sure, I had a million T-shirts, jeans, skirts, all sorts of things. But nothing in my wardrobe was what I considered worthy of the occasion.

"Uh, Julie?" I said, weakly.

"Sugar? What's up?" She was, by this time, vacuuming the living room. She switched off the vacuum cleaner and looked at me expectantly.

"I have... I have nothing to wear."

Jillian chose that moment to walk in. She screeched. I wasn't sure whether she was horrified that she was related to me, or thrilled that I was finally showing interest in something besides the colour and texture of the ceiling paint.

"That's wonderful!" Julie yelled.

Jillian dropped her bags by the kitchen door and hurried out to the living room. "Oh, baby!" I was engulfed in a spicy patchouli hug.

"Let's go immediately. We can pick up some things at the mall in a hurry." She turned to Julie. "You have—"

Julie waved us off with a huge grin. "Go before she changes her mind."

Jillian and I got into the car and sped to the mall in record time. She practically dragged me into a store called Sweet Harts, which had half-naked mannequins all over showing legs and boobs and bellies and butts to an alarming degree. I never would have expected her to choose this store, and not these clothes, given the way she dressed herself. Then I remembered seeing pictures of her the way she used to look in her teens, before she left Trinidad. She was pretty and girlish and prone to frills.

"Uh, Aunty," I stammered out.

She didn't hear me. She had a tube top in one hand and a miniskirt in the other and was sizing me up with a glance that made me feel a little afraid.

"Aunty! I don't think this is my speed," I said, more firmly.

Her face fell. I was wearing a plain black T-shirt, black joggers and Birkenstocks at the time. While I wasn't ready to meet the most gorgeous boy in the world looking like that, I sure wasn't going to meet him with my boobs hanging out.

"Of course, baby," she said, ruefully putting the clothes back on their hangers and turning for the exit.

Back in the mall way, I spotted another store. Regular jeans and shirts were on the mannequins in this window.

"What if we try this one?" I said.

We walked around in there and still there wasn't anything I liked. Nothing screamed *This is What to Wear to Meet the Most Gorgeous Boy in the World*.

In the third store we hit the jackpot. It was a soft lilac dress; Aunt Jillian said it had cap sleeves and an empire waistline, falling in an A-line skirt just below my knees. It wasn't too girly girl but it wasn't severe, either. Against my dark skin it looked divine. The Birkenstocks didn't look so hot with it, though. And the socks definitely had to go.

"We need to get you some sandals. I mean nice sandals," she said, grimacing at the Birkenstocks. They were comfy and practical but not exactly cute.

I got some white sandals with low heels. They fitted okay, though not as comfortably as the clunky Birkenstocks. But these sandals were pretty. They made my toes look long and elegant, I noted with pride and some awe. Jillian was so excited about the whole ensemble I didn't have the heart to tell her I planned to wear the dress over a pair of skinny jeans.

On the way out we passed a kiosk with cosmetics. I lagged behind and Jillian gave in with mock exasperation. A tube of lip-gloss later, we were out in the car and speeding back home.

People started coming over at about two in the afternoon. Jillian fired up the big grill on the deck in the warm sunshine and Julie laid out some chips and salads while the meat sizzled.

By four o'clock the place was full. A blur of faces passed me by. I stuck to the living room, playing DJ with Julie's iPad and with an aux cord connecting it to the stereo system. I was reading the track list on a Prince greatest hits collection when I heard a husky voice say hello.

I jumped about a foot.

He was wearing a white T-shirt and black skinny jeans strategically ripped at the knees. He had on a bandana, too, tied like a headband. He looked like a young thug. I was a little disappointed. The boys I knew at home who dressed like that usually had nothing to say except dumb things they picked up off of hip hop and dancehall music, stuff they didn't really understand the ramifications of but repeated because So-and-So said it in some song.

His next words, therefore, came as a complete surprise to me.

"Oh, snap! Is that a greatest hits? See if it has 'I Wanna Be Your Lover' on it. Oh, man. That is the baddest love song, ever. RIP to The Artist."

"RIP," I murmured back. I was thinking that I didn't know if I agreed with him on that song's position as the greatest love song ever. In fact, I think I definitely disagreed with him. But who would have thought that he would know the works of my favourite singer? Not me. I was thrilled.

Okay, maybe Prince wasn't my *very* favourite singer. But he was up there with the top ones.

"You like Prince?"

"Oh, yeah. No doubt. He was the best musician of his time, bar none," he said, stooping to my level, literally if not metaphorically. Taking the iPad from me, he read off the titles on the album's playlist. "You gotta run this track!" he said, pointing to 'When Doves Cry' on the list. "I have loved this since I was a kid watching that old movie with my mom. She watches it every year."

Hmm. You never know about people from just looking at them.

I must have looked at him funny because he suddenly got self-conscious. "What?" he asked.

"Uh. Nothing." We played the music.

During the next twenty minutes we said maybe five words to each other, but it was a friendly kind of silence. My aunt came in with Nathan.

"You kids having fun? Can we get something other than Prince now?"

"One more song," Joshua and I said at the very same time, breaking into laughter as we said it.

"One more!" Nathan sighed. "There must be something else you guys can agree on."

"How about this?" Joshua, who had been rifling through iTunes, highlighted Santana's *Supernatural*. I raised an eyebrow and nodded approvingly. He had good taste in music as far as I was concerned. But I wasn't entirely convinced; could be he was making the best of a bad situation and didn't really like this stuff. It was just that the most recent dancehall Jillian had was some Super Cat circa 1990, and as for hip hop, *The Miseducation of Lauryn Hill* was the most up to date of the lot. Her tastes ranged to the old and romantic, rather than the young and urban. She had a lot of folk and jazz music, some calypso and, of course, Bob Marley, which was practically a prerequisite for any music collection. But the stuff that I listened to at home—Rihanna, Beyoncé, Drake, The Weeknd, Popcaan, Kendrick Lamar, Machel Montano, Bunji Garlin—was conspicuously absent from her iTunes list.

I seemed to be wrong in my judgment of Joshua's tastes. He continued to pull stuff out that gave further lie to his gangsta uniform. The Beatles, Simon & Garfunkel, Earth, Wind and Fire and Parliament Funk joined Santana in a growing playlist. His sparkling grey-green eyes squinted in concentration as he checked out more music. I got to my feet and stretched. "Hey, want some sweetdrink?" I asked.

"Huh?"

"Soda. Pop. Want some?"

"Yeah, sure. Coke, if you have it. What did you call it?"

"Sweetdrink. I pronounced it *seejink*, the way we usually did home home. It's what my mom always calls it. It's a Trini thing, you wouldn't understand."

"Sure I would," he scoffed. "Unnu nah recognize me a fi 'alf Jamaican, mon?" It was a pretty bad accent but he seemed proud of it. I remembered that his mom lived in the States. He'd probably never seen Jamaica.

"Riiiight," I said. "Let me get that Coke."

Julie was in the kitchen, wearing an apron that said, "Kiss the cook," so I did.

"You're in a good mood," she observed as I poured two glasses of soda.

Santana's old duet with Rob Thomas, 'Smooth' came on. "Uh huh, I sure am! We're playing back-in-times music," I said, as I did a little three-step.

Julie grimaced in fake agony. "Is this considered 'back-in-times' already? God, I'm old. How are the burgers?" There was a tall stack of them next to her. Red meat wasn't a big mover that afternoon; all the bean patties and other vegan stuff were gone already. I gathered up a paper plate of three actual meat burgers along with the drinks. It was a precarious arrangement. As soon as Joshua saw me carrying the wobbling freight, he sprang to his feet and took the plate and a glass from me.

"Hope you eat beef," I told him. I settled next to him and bit into my sandwich. Burger juice spurted out and spattered on my lap, right on my new dress. "Oh, man!" I whined. Now I'd have to change it. And of course, I had nothing else to wear.

"Oh, come on, it's just a little spot," he said, whipping off his bandana and dabbing at it. It was cute. I was blushing so hard I was nearly glowing. He unfolded the bandana and draped it on my lap like a napkin. "So you don't mess up your nice outfit any more," he added.

He thought my outfit was nice? *Yay!*

We listened to more music, talking little, and ate some chips and salsa. By nine o'clock his dad came around again. Nathan was pretty drunk, by the sound of it. He slurred his words a lot and took much longer to finish his sentences than usual. He also had a glass of wine in hand.

"Looks like I'm spending the night here," Joshua said. "Hope your couch is comfortable."

The way he said it made me feel he had been in this position before, but I didn't want to ask. I didn't have to, as it turned out.

"He's drunk a lot these days. He's breaking up with his girlfriend." He shook his head. "Man, you must be so glad your aunts are in a stable relationship."

Hearing the words coming from his mouth made me feel a bit surreal. These aren't things we talk about at *home home*. I thought that, at home, Jillian and Julie's relationship would have been probably passed off as just a close friendship. And no matter how drunk somebody's dad was, nobody would have ever said a word.

"It sucks that my dad is in this up and down thing. I never know if she's going to be at the apartment when I get home or not. Talk about a bad connection."

"I'm sorry."

"Yeah," Joshua said. "It kind of sucks. I only get to see him once a year and he doesn't realise that he's wasting our two months together by being drunk all the time."

"You dad has been drunk for two months?" I asked, incredulous. That sounded a bit intense.

"Well," he reconsidered, "maybe not every day. But often. At least he doesn't get violent or anything, just mopey. I have to hear about every girlfriend he's ever had when he gets into it," he said, with a little laugh, shaking his head. "Your aunt Jillian was the one that got away." He paused, passing his hands idly through his curly hair and momentarily distracting me from our very serious conversation. "How do you like living with your aunts, anyway? Julie told us the other night that you might be moving here permanently."

My heart skipped a beat. I might be moving here *permanently*? It was news to me. I shoved the thought aside for the moment. It was too distracting. Instead I focused on answering his question. "I don't know. I like it a lot, I guess. But I haven't been to school yet, and it's not like real life, you know? I don't have any friends here."

I paused. Mentally I added to myself that I didn't have any friends at home, either. Akilah was the only one I could talk to without feeling like a complete extraterrestrial. I just had nothing in common with most of the kids I knew.

As if she had heard her name called in my mind half a world away, the bubbling ringtone announced a Skype call from Akilah. I excused myself and took the call in the bathroom.

The first thing I did when I answered was to shriek silently. Akilah saw me freaking out and was immediately worried. "What? What? What?"

"Relax," I said. "It's just that I'm. With. The. Boy."

"What!!!"

"Oh my God, you have to meet him. Ki-ki!! Help me! I don't know what to say! I'm so dumb and awkward. What if he—"

Akilah interrupted my rant right there. "Come on, silly. You're not dumb. Awkward, yes. But that's where I come in. Let's go meet your boyfriend," she teased. I took the phone back to the living room and introduced Akilah to Joshua.

"Hey, nice to meet you," he said in that very velvety voice.

When I turned the phone back to myself Akilah's expression showed that she was very impressed with Josh, very impressed indeed. She gave me two thumbs up. I made *monkey face*, sticking out my tongue and waggling it enthusiastically.

"What?" Joshua asked, grinning but obviously puzzled. I guess monkey face is not a good look for me. *Darn it.*

"Babes, it's really loud out there," Akilah complained.

"Can we go to your room or something?" Joshua suggested.

We sat on the floor beside the bed.

"So," Akilah broke the silence, "how did you guys meet?"

Josh told her the story. He left out the part about how I got sick in the middle of dinner. She already knew about it, though. He turned to look at me. His eyes were smiling – "Smizing", like Tyra Banks calls it on her TV show with the models. "I'm glad my dad is friends with your aunts," he concluded. I blushed so hard and immediately changed the subject.

"I really need someone to talk to about my situation with Julie and Jillian. They are great but it weirds me out sometimes to know that they are a couple. Like they have *sex and stuff*," I confessed to Josh and Akilah.

"Hashtag *country bookie*!" Akilah said.

"What is a 'country bookie'?" asked Josh.

"That is what Trinidadians call a bumpkin," I jumped in.

Akilah continued, "Josh, to be honest, where we come from you never see a gay couple. And if you see one, you'll never see them kiss in public. There are places where that will earn you and your lover a beat down, for reals."

"True?" he murmured. "I hear things like that about Jamaica but I never went there."

"Can I ask you something?" I asked. He glanced up at me with those stunning eyes. I melted a little inside but then steeled myself to continue to talk about my living situation. "It's great. They're great. But I just don't know how to feel about them being. Well, you know."

He raised an eyebrow and lifted his palms in puzzlement.

I sighed. "You know. *Gay.*" I said it low, spat it out like a bad word.

Akilah cackled on her end of the phone call. "You can say the word, chile! I know you can! Say it loud, say it proud!"

We all laughed, and then Joshua said seriously. "You can say *gay*. Kids I know say *queer* sometimes. Gay is not a bad word. It doesn't change who people are, if they're gay or straight. Take my dad. He's not much of a dad, and that doesn't have anything to do with whether he's gay or straight. You just have to accept people for who they are and who they love."

"That's easy for you to say. Where I'm from, you just don't say those things out loud. I can't think of one single gay couple at home, not even like a celebrity couple. I don't know. People just hide it. For me this is… Boom! Mind. Blown." With my hands I mimed my head exploding. We all laughed again.

"It's not important, trust me." He looked over at me meaningfully. "Can I tell you something?"

I nodded.

"My mom has had a boyfriend but when I was little she had a girlfriend. Some of the times she seemed the happiest were with her girlfriend, I think. Being gay or bi or whatever doesn't change who she is or how she treats me. That's the important thing: your aunts love you, don't they? And they show it." He looked frustrated, and fiddled with his own phone as he talked. "I just wish my dad was more… caring. Sounds dumb, coming from a guy, right?"

"Are you gay?" Akilah joked lamely.

He glared. "That's not funny."

"Yeah, I know. Sorry." She looked abashed. He grinned and waved it away.

Then we were all friends.

Chapter

Josh and Nathan weren't the only ones staying overnight. A couple of other people did, too. Most of the adults stayed up late into the night, taking over the living room, drinking wine or coffee and watching movies. As expected, some ended up sleeping on the carpet, and some on the sofabed.

We talked to Akilah for hours. He had music on his phone and I had a Bluetooth speaker so we listened to some tunes on his SoundCloud. It was mostly hip hop and dancehall, but there were some rock and dance tunes in there too. (Akilah ratted me out, telling him that I liked Justin Bieber and he said he understood and didn't think I was a bad person. My heart sang.)

"What's your school like?" Akilah asked him.

"Oh, normal. You know."

"Well, actually, I don't. Remember I live in Trinidad. School there is much different from what I see on American TV."

He laughed out loud. "School everywhere is different from what you see on American TV. Nobody looks *that* good."

I refrained from pointing out that he looked like a super-cute extra on *The Vampire Diaries*.

He continued, "I'm a senior at Audre Lorde Charter School."

"Where's that?" Akilah was asking all the questions I wanted to ask but was too shy to speak out loud.

"Oh, in New York."

"Duh," she said. We cracked up again.

"Brooklyn, to be specific. Close to where my mom and I live. It's okay, I guess. I'm doing a bunch of pre-pre-law stuff, like the constitution and society, for extra credit. I'm applying to Columbia and I want to go to law school there eventually… but I don't know if I'm going to transfer and spend a year up here with my dad before college." He turned those hazel eyes on me. "What about you?"

"I'm in third form, which is like"—I did some quick maths in my head— "about ninth grade?"

"You're that young?" he said, surprised. "Thought you were about sixteen."

I ducked my head. "Nah. Fifteen in two months. I'm kind of tall for my age."

"You can say that again! How tall are you?"

"A little under six foot," I said.

"With that height and your looks, how come you're not a model? If you lived in New York you would have been spotted by now."

"I know, right?" Akilah yelled. "She's so pretty and she doesn't even know it."

"Oh, please," I said.

"No, seriously. You're really pretty," Josh repeated Akilah's assurances.

I turned away. A boy had never called me pretty before. Tall, skinny, dark girls with short hair didn't get called pretty where I came from.

Josh could see I didn't believe him.

"Tell me you're kidding," he said.

Again I said nothing.

Akilah sucked her teeth, frustrated. "I've been telling her that forever but she never believes me."

"Okay, but don't say I didn't tell her so." He let it drop and turned back to me. "Tell me about your school."

"Well," I said, "I do boring stuff. English, Spanish, social studies, integrated science, geography. It's co-ed. The boys do electrical stuff and woodwork and the girls do sewing and cooking. We could do it vice versa but nobody really encourages you to do that, so we stick with tradition. It's not considered a good school but it's okay. I mean, it's kind of rough."

"Kinda?" Akilah jumped in. "With some guys selling weed behind the technical block, and some girls getting into fights… they stab each other over boyfriends and stuff."

"Fights… like with *knives*?" he asked.

"Yeah. It's rough. But it could be worse: they could have guns," Akilah said, deadpan.

"It's okay, it's not that bad," I said, desperate to stop talking about it.

"Wow. Why don't your parents put you in a different school?"

"Parent," I corrected. "My mom's a single parent. Never had a dad, actually." He nodded but didn't say anything, waiting for me to continue. "And with school, well, it's not that easy to move kids around from school to school," I said. "There's this assessment exam you have to do to get into a high school and I failed."

"You didn't fail!" Akilah squawked.

"Okay, true, I didn't fail, I just didn't do well enough to go to a great school. My mom thinks I should live with the *consequences of my actions*." I did a good imitation of my mother's serious voice as I put bunny ears around the words she had so often said. *Bitter much, kiddo?* I asked myself.

"So she'd rather you went to a school you didn't like, where there are drug dealers and violent gangs, so you could live with the consequence of your actions? Sounds crazy," he said.

When he said it like that, I had to agree with him. But I had to stick up for my mom. "She means well."

"Besides," said Akilah, "those schools are where the majority of kids end up in our country. It's normal."

"Uh huh." He didn't sound convinced.

"It's not that serious," I said, trying to be casual. "Can we talk about what you heard from your dad? That I might be here permanently?"

Akilah gasped. "Oh no! You have to come home!"

"Yuck," I said, gagging dramatically. "I hate that place." Though I realised it was only partly true.

"No, you don't," she rejoined.

"What is there to like?" I said. "Oh yeah, I can't wait to get back to the country where there's more than one murder every day."

"Really?" Josh was shocked. "In such a small place?"

"Yeah," Akilah reluctantly agreed. "Crime is terrible. As a girl nobody wants you out at night by yourself. They say you could get kidnapped, sold into the sex trade."

"For real?" His widened eyes were joined by a gaping mouth. "I knew that kind of thing happens in big cities like New York, not in the Caribbean."

"Or how about the truly loveable public utilities?" I grumbled. "We get power outages... how often, Ki-ki?"

"Once a month, maybe," she allowed.

"Wow, when the lights go out in New York it makes the news," Josh said.

"And let's not talk about water."

"What do you mean, water?" Josh asked.

Akilah fielded that one. "You know how you open the tap and water comes out when you pay your bill? Well where we come from, most of the country doesn't get water when it opens its taps. Not every day, anyway."

"Tuesdays and Saturdays," I added. "That's when we get water in my neighbourhood. All the rest of the week we have to use water from the tanks."

"And what if your tank is empty?" Josh asked.

"Salt," Akilah said.

"What?" I don't understand what you mean by 'salt'," Josh admitted.

"It means you get nothing. Nada. Salt. It means, 'You can use the bathroom at the mall, because they have water and you can't flush your toilet'," Akilah clarified.

He shuddered. "It isn't all that bad, you're exaggerating."

"I wish," I said, bitterly.

Akilah replied, "It can be really bad here. But it's beautiful too," she chided me. "Come on, admit it!"

"Well," I said, "the hills are kinda spectacular. And the people are great. Sometimes."

"When they're not trying to kill gay people?" Josh asked sarcastically. "Your country sounds lovely. I can't imagine why you'd ever leave."

"But it's home, you know?" Akilah said. "I couldn't leave. For all its faults it is an amazing place. There's so much passion and creativity. The land and sea are beautiful. And the people—we are gorgeous, you have to admit." She winked at Josh, and he smiled back goofily. I rolled my eyes at them. Akilah finished, "We make it work and it's where I belong."

I thought about that for a second. Was it where I belonged?

Josh changed the topic, turning to look at me. "My mom sounds like the opposite to your mom. She's really over-protective of me. I had to go to the best school—it's public but a charter school, which is like a private public school… it's hard to explain," he ended, looking at my confused expression. "Whatever. It's a good school, no knives—or guns. But, like I said, I really want to spend some time with my dad before I start college."

"Have you ever lived with him before?" I asked.

"Yeah, when I was a baby, I guess," Joshua said, picking at imaginary lint on his jeans. "But I don't remember it. I only know him from spending summers with him every year. It's harder because I live in the States and he lives all the way up here. This place is like *The Boonies*, man. And it's sooooo white!"

"For reals!" I chimed in. At home we'd be just faces in the crowd—in Joshua's case a gorgeous face in the crowd. But we of the brown skin stick out somewhat in Edmonton compared to the multicultural places Josh and I come from. For a few minutes we all traded tales about Trinidad and Brooklyn, and about Caribbean, African, Latin American and other brown-skinned folks in general.

Josh sighed, "It's nice to get a break from my mom, too." He bit his lip, hesitating, before he spoke again. "She's depressed and it's like, every day is a drama. Sometimes." He quickly added, as if he didn't want to be disloyal to her even in her absence, "I love her a lot, you know? But it's kind of tough to be around her twenty-four-seven."

I turned it over in my mind for all of two seconds before I jumped to his mom's defence—a woman I'd never met. "I'm sure she's trying her best. Depression isn't easy to cope with. I know."

"Yeah, it's tough. But she makes it harder. She doesn't go to her therapist, she drinks too much sometimes, she skips taking her meds. She's a great mom but I just wish she'd realise that all that stuff—the medication, the therapy, the yoga—is actually good for her, and not just something we're forcing her to do because we hate her."

Akilah's mother yelled at her for being on the phone too long. Ki-ki made her apologies and rang off, promising to talk to me again the next day.

Josh and I continued to talk about his mom. "What's she taking?" I asked. "Some of the medication can have awful side effects, you know. It can make you fat, sleepy, dopey."

"Uh huh, I know," he muttered, looking at me strangely. "She's on Prozac. She says it messes with her sex drive. How come you know so much about this?"

"How come you think?" I asked, darkly.

"Oh snap! You too?"

I nodded, without looking at him. I didn't want to see the look on his face.

"Hey," he said, awkward but gentle, "it's cool. I mean, I know you're not like, you know, *crazy crazy*. It's cool."

I snuck a glance at him. "For reals?"

"Yeah," he said, a small smile on his sweet lips.

Not only was he cute and smart, he had great taste in music, and he was understanding, too.

"At least you think so. People at home would never understand. If it ever came out in school that I had attempted suicide, that I was clinically depressed and living with a chronic mental illness, I would be persecuted relentlessly," I confided. "Where I come from a lot of people think mental illness is either demon possession or deliberate bad behaviour."

"Are you serious?"

"Yeah," I said. "My own mom… she thinks I'm just being over-dramatic."

My mother's attitude was, sadly, typical: I felt I could count on one finger the number of people at home who would be sympathetic to someone with a mental illness. And did Akilah really count in this equation? She was a kid like me. She couldn't protect me.

We talked more, listening to some of Josh's favourite music. He was deeply into trap, the strange, hectic hip hop music from the southern US. I knew some trap songs, the ones that had made it to the radio at home, but I wasn't really a fan. He played his favourites and explained as well as he could what the songs were about—many of them were about selling drugs, but not all of them.

"I don't get it," I finally admitted.

"Word," he said, grinning. "You don't have to. We can like different things and still be cool." I fiddled with my fingers. He took one of my hands in his. "Are you nervous?"

My heart was in my throat. Joshua's hands were warm, soft, strong. Next to his light brown skin mine seemed extra dark. I didn't know what to do. Should I sit there with my hand limp? Should I touch him with my other hand? *What should I do? What?*

Akilah and I had strategised about this. She had raised the possibility that he might try to kiss me. I had wanted to dismiss it completely but she had insisted. Boys are boys, no matter where they are from, she said, and he's going to try to kiss you if he likes you and you two are alone. Her advice was to "be natural". Since I'd never kissed a boy (or a girl, for that matter), I had no idea what "natural" looked like in this context. My heartbeat raced like *tassa* drumming.

Weakly I tried to pull my hand from Joshua's grasp but he held on and gave me a tug in the opposite direction, pulling me up to sit on the bed. We faced each other with our legs folded like yogis, his sneakers taken off long ago and parked by the bedroom door, and my sandals tossed beside them. His eyes were lasers, pinning me down. He leaned towards me and I could smell his cologne, something fresh and breezy, and his breath, minty from the gum we had chewed after finishing our burgers. I closed my eyes.

His lips barely, delicately touched mine.

And then the door swung open. "Oops!" Nathan chortled, more amused than apologetic for barging in on us at this key moment. "Sorry to interrupt! Josh, I just wanted to let you know we are definitely staying the night."

Hastily pulling away from each other, Joshua and I dropped our hands into our laps and looked at Nathan innocently.

"Sure, Dad," Joshua mumbled.

"Hey, no funny stuff, okay?" Nathan teased his son, stepping into the room and ruffling his curls. "I know she's beautiful but you have to let her get to know you first, son," he teased. I could tell he was drunk, but under the slurred words and cloud of alcohol fumes I could also tell there was a spark of parental concern. "I don't want her to break your heart." Nathan theatrically winked at me before stumbling out of the room again.

Our moment was over. We turned back to the music. I stayed seated on the bed and he sat on the floor. We were further apart than before… but he was holding my hand.

I woke up the next morning with a crusty feeling in my mouth and a great big smile on my face. Joshua's curly hair was just visible under a drift of blankets on the floor next to my bed. Through the open door I heard the blessed sound of silence. I was evidently the first awake. Or maybe not. I heard the sound of water running in the kitchen and bet myself that Julie was up and cleaning the mess left over from the party.

Climbing over Joshua's inert body, I crept out to get a glass of juice from the fridge. Just as I suspected, Julie was scrubbing away at the counters, getting rid of a vicious maroon stain next to the sink.

"Bloody red wine," she muttered as I walked in. "Hey, muffin. How was your little party?" she asked with a tiny smirk.

I felt my cheeks blaze. "Oh, it wasn't like that," I started to explain.

She laughed, swatting me with a damp tea towel. "I should hope not! I was kidding, honey. I'm glad you're making a friend. I was worried that you'd never talk to anybody outside this family ever again." Her teasing smile was gentle. I felt happy and excited and couldn't wait to tell her about the whole thing.

"We just played music. Talked. He's really nice," I said. I wanted to explain more, about how easy he was to talk to, how he understood about my depression. *How we sort of kissed. Almost.* But the words were caught up in my chest and wouldn't come out. Instead, I mumbled again, "He's really nice."

Her smile told me she understood.

I poured my juice and drank it, feeling my stomach beginning to rumble with hunger. I glanced at the clock on the microwave and was surprised to see it was after eight already.

"If I were back home I would have been in church by now, just starting mass," I told Julie. "Mom insists we go to church every week, and I don't even know why. It's not as though she's all that devout."

"Maybe she likes the routine of it?" Julie asked. "The predictability?"

I could kind of understand that; I liked order, too. But I didn't see the point of going to church if you didn't want to be a real Christian and were just doing it for form's sake. To me, it seemed like a waste of time—but maybe that was just me. I shrugged.

I turned back to the fridge, opened the door and did a fridge stare, trying to figure out what was quick and easy for me to have for breakfast.

"Here," said Julie, reaching around me to grab a stack of cheese slices from the dairy compartment and a bag of English muffins from a packed shelf. "I'll toast one for you."

"Julie, can I ask you something about Jillian?"

She responded with a cautious nod. "But really if you have something you want to know you should ask Jillian herself. She won't bite," she teased.

I was finishing off the crisp, warm bread with melted cheese when Joshua's dad came in, wearing a T-shirt and boxers. He was stretching and yawning and scratching, looking like a man from a movie, so stereotypically crass and obviously hung over. If I wasn't sure before, I was convinced then that I didn't like him much.

"Morning, ladies," he said, in between huge yawns. "Julie, what has your niece done with my son?"

While they talked I took the opportunity to use the bathroom, washing my face and brushing my teeth and generally trying to look slightly less jacked up than I had when I crawled out of bed.

I needn't have worried. Joshua was still fast asleep when I tiptoed back into the bedroom. In fact, he slept until nearly noon. His dad woke him up just before it was time for them to drive back home. He only had time to give me a quick hug before slipping away and driving off in his dad's car. I thought I'd probably see him again soon. I hoped I would, anyway.

When Akilah called we did an exhaustive analysis of the whole three-way conversation, and then further discussed every second of the almost-kiss and the hand-holding that followed it. We agreed we'd have to wait until the next time I saw Josh to deliberate further.

That week drifted by with me staying mostly at home, listening to music, watching movies from Jillian's enormous collection and surfing the net. I toyed with the idea of starting a new Instagram account, but then changed my mind. I wasn't ready yet to do anything so public. Instead I contented myself with obsessively watching Buzzfeed videos on YouTube. I was too scared to ask Aunt Jillian to get his number from his dad for me, but I held on to the memory of the way Josh and I had almost kissed.

I was starting to feel like the world wasn't such a bad place.

Then my mom called again. From the airport.

Chapter
9

Though I wanted to go into hiding and never come out, Jillian and Julie made me go with them to meet my mom.

"Cynthia!" yelled Jillian, pleased as punch to see her sister. Jillian's last trip home had been ages ago, like I said, and they hadn't seen each other since. My trip into exile had been planned over phone calls; I was out of hospital one day and in the air the next, flying as a terrified unaccompanied minor to my recovery in Edmonton.

Mom was looking really pert and pretty in jeans and a crisp white shirt. I guess having no child to look after suited her to the bone. It was all right by me, since being away from her suited me just fine, too.

The airport was a cavernous, frightening place, like a cross between a market and the super mall. It had a huge, high ceiling, with ranks of uncomfortable-looking plastic chairs and miserable passengers dragging enormous suitcases around and looking like they were lost. In between, there were flight crews pulling smart black carry-on cases on wheels, striding purposefully from one end of the airport to the next. Though it was daytime, neon lights lit the book, candy and souvenir stores. A stuffed horse made of fluffy plush fabric called my name, but I didn't stop to say hello, just threw it a longing look before trailing after Jillian and Julie to greet Mom.

Her hug was stiff. Our dialogue was just like I had imagined it would be:

How are you?

Fine. You?

Fine.

How is everything at home?

Fine.

It took all of ten seconds, probably, to run out of things to say. *Yes, I was taking my medication. No, I wasn't feeling ill. Yes, the doctor said I was improving. No, I didn't miss home. At all,* I lied.

I guess she was a bit perturbed that I would come right out and admit that I was happier in Canada than at home, but she didn't say anything. I supposed I was in for it later on, though. To my surprise I felt some anxiety when I saw her, but nothing like the rushing-to-my-doom overwhelming despair that would normally have accompanied such a meeting just a couple of months ago. In fact, I could honestly say that I really felt… fine. I hoped it would last.

She didn't have much luggage, just one suitcase, which Julie quickly grabbed from her and hauled off to the car. We took Mom to lunch at a steakhouse and she and Jillian made conversation about everything at home and how everyone was doing. Mom kept staring at Julie from time to time, and I wanted to kick her for making Julie seem like some kind of freak, but Julie handled it like a pro, neither ignoring Mom nor pointedly staring back. I felt a bit bad at first, but as the evening progressed I got more and more angry.

It had been about two months since I had seen my mother. The time had changed us both, I realised.

She and Jillian were laughing over some old schoolteacher they had had when I interrupted without preamble.

"I don't want to go back."

Julie immediately tried to play it off. "Hey, muffin, we can talk about that later…"

Mom wasn't having that, though. She engaged without missing a beat.

"It's time for you to get back to your real life. You have to go back to school. Your place is at home."

"My *real life* is in a place where nobody wants me around, nobody understands me and nobody really cares if I live or die?" I asked, the light of challenge sparking in my dark eyes.

My mother was outraged. "What nonsense! What self-indulgent nonsense! Of course we care about you! We might not always understand you, granted, but we always do our best by you, child. How dare you come with this attitude, these accusations?"

Jillian tried to calm the turbulent waters. "Cynthia, you know she's just exaggerating. Of course we all know you care about her and whether she lives or dies. She's not being literal. I just think she means that she doesn't feel accepted for who she is."

My mother's mouth was a thin, unsmiling line. "Who she is, is my daughter. Her place is at home, with me. Whether I *understand* or *accept* her or not."

The waiter came with the bill and Jillian tersely handed him a credit card before turning back to her little sister. "I really think it's bigger than that, Cynthia. You have to understand that she's ill, she has an illness that requires her to be loved and accepted or she'll be worse off—"

Mom snorted. Clearly, despite all the doctors we had talked to after my pill-popping incident, she wasn't convinced I was actually ill. As far as she was concerned depression was some kind of self-induced and entirely frivolous condition. In other words, I was probably making all this up. Furthermore, I was making all this up to spite her.

Nothing was further from the truth. But I knew I couldn't

convince Mom over steak and salad.

The ride back to the house was tense. Over the stiff silence, Jillian and Julie pointed out landmarks to Mom's stony face, and I *steupsed* under my breath a couple of times before Jillian told me to cut it out. Sucking your teeth to an adult was a no-no here too, it seemed. Finally we were home. We pulled into our street just as a bus roared off in a cloud of hot air.

Mom got out of the car with a flounce, walked around and stood by the trunk tapping her foot impatiently. She was in a hurry to finish the discussion. So was I. Jillian wasn't, though. She eased the suitcase out of the trunk and up the steps to the front door and into the immaculate living room. Julie and Jillian gave her a quick tour, ending at my bedroom. Jillian left Cynthia's suitcase in my room, although my mom would sleep on the fold-out living-room couch during her visit—her choice, even though she could have slept with me in the guest room. Mom glanced around at the small room, painted a pale pink, with its white anglaise cotton curtains and comforter and white furniture. It was a girl's room; it occurred to me for the first time that they had probably decorated it for me just before I got to Edmonton. I could see, from the tightness around her mouth, that the thought had occurred to my mother at the same time it did me.

I saw her eyes flicking over the neat room and knew she was mentally comparing it to my room at home, which was even smaller and was never this neat. I kept this room tidy because, even though Jillian was family, I wasn't really at *home home* and didn't want her to feel put upon by my presence any more than was necessary. Somehow I wanted to make the best possible impression, in spite of everything. My mother, who knew me from before I was born, would have understood all that without me saying anything, and I saw something flicker in her eyes as she took in the room, the neatly stacked books on the night table, the absence of clothes strewn on the crisply made bed. Even the floor was clean, with no shoes thrown haphazardly around as they would have been back home. She looked at me, that same unreadable expression in her eyes, looked back at the room and walked out without a word.

It was hours before bedtime and we had yet to talk about the purpose of her visit: to take me home.

I've never seen my mother cry. She's just not the crying type; she'd quicker hit you than let you see her weak or wounded. I think that part of what she never accepted about my illness was that it seemed like weakness to her. Mom expected everyone to be able to just *deal*. Lonely? Deal with it. Man left you? Deal with it. Hate your job? Deal with it. Don't break down, don't trip. Just quietly and efficiently deal with whatever it is bothering you. Deal with it and shut up. I'd tried her method. It made me want to die. Everybody isn't wired the same way.

Jillian led the way to the deck while Julie went into the kitchen to get everyone some cold drinks. It was afternoon, warm and muggy by Canadian standards, which after two months had suddenly, it seemed, become my standards. I didn't know how I would cope when I went back home to the furnace-like heat and ponderously humid air. My hair, cut so short when I had come, had grown out a bit into a wiry Afro, sort of like Jillian's, but thicker. I took a hank of the tight strands and started twirling it between my fingers and thumb, making little curls that stuck out from my head at right angles. I could tell from Mom's disdainful look that she didn't appreciate the aesthetic, but it wasn't meant to be a fashion statement, just something to do with my hands.

"Have you been keeping up with your school work?" she asked, checking out the pristine lawn and pretty flowers as she talked.

"Not really," I admitted. "I go to the library a lot but mostly I just read whatever I feel like, not on any particular subject. I am teaching myself French, though," I added.

"French?" Frowning, she turned back to me.

"You didn't tell me that," said Jillian, with a surprised grin. "I could have helped. *J'adore le Français*," she said, with the requisite guttural inflections.

I saw my mom tighten her mouth, so I changed the subject. "I bought a dress," I said. "Want to see it?"

She looked wounded. Too late, I reflected that she had tried for years to get me to care enough about my appearance to buy a dress of my own accord—with no success whatever. And now, here, I've finally done it. Without her.

The afternoon wasn't going well.

Julie came out, as fresh as summer flowers, carrying glasses of lemonade on a tray. She was such a domestic type, it was almost funny, a real Wilma Flintstone. Not that Jillian was flat-footed Fred to her Wilma, just that Julie was so concerned with keeping things running clean and smooth. I envied her easy way with both housekeeping and people. Remembering how she effortlessly handled Nathan in his caveman wake-up mode, I admired once again her ability to smooth people's feathers as she graciously handed my mom her glass of lemonade, doing a little dip at the knees to keep the waiter steady.

"Oh, look at you with your bunny dip," Jillian teased her.

I was confused. Bunny? Seeing my confusion, Jillian explained.

"Julie used to be a waitress in Toronto for a while at this gentleman's club—"

"—Read: strip club," interjected Julie.

"—and they taught her how to do something called the 'bunny dip,' so she could serve drinks without bending over and showing her cleavage," Jillian said.

"Yeah, showing cleavage was strictly reserved for the girls on the poles," Julie joked.

"The move was invented by the Playboy Bunnies, for their club," Jillian ended.

My mother was less and less amused as the moments ticked by. "You worked in a strip club?" She made it sound like Julie had made a living selling crack outside a kindergarten or something.

"It was only for a couple of months, when I was an undergrad," Julie said. I liked how she said it without tension, as if there were nothing to be ashamed about. As if it were just a job.

Mom's top lip was curling further and further into a sneer. "Doesn't sound like a great place for a woman to work," she said.

"Actually," Julie replied, "it wasn't a bad place at all. Management was very strict about customers not being able to touch the employees. And the tips were great," she threw in with a wink.

As fascinated as I was by the idea of strip clubs and bunny dips, I was anxious to get to the meat of the discussion. So was my mother, apparently. She cut to the chase.

"Jillian, it's time for this child to come home with me."

There were tears in my eyes.

I couldn't help it. I was sad, angry, frustrated, but mostly horrified at the thought of going home. I just wasn't ready yet to face the same old places where nobody cared about me, the school where I didn't fit in. In any case, hardly anybody tried to actually teach us anything there; they had given up on us before we had even started. As a school clerk herself, my mother ought to have known that but she didn't seem to care much whether I did well or didn't, whether the school I went to was good, bad or indifferent, whether the kids I sat next to in class were going to grow up to be pharmacists or drug dealers. If she cared, she did an awful lot not to show it. If she cared, she was awfully good at pretending otherwise.

It wasn't just the school. I didn't hate it all the time; it was okay some days. It wasn't anything specific that made me unhappy there. And it wasn't really her. It was the whole country—the smallness of it—that seemed to close in on me sometimes. I could understand why some LGBT people like Jillian couldn't really be comfortable living in a small place like that, where to be gay or lesbian was a shameful secret you could hint at but never discuss, not openly. So to them at home Jillian was a spinster, but in fact she was as good as married to a woman who was her life partner, with whom she kept a nice house and who loved Jillian as much as Jillian loved her. *Home home* was full of people like my mother who couldn't separate a person from their sexual and domestic arrangements—which weren't really their business anyway—and whose judgment was flawed regarding anything they couldn't understand. To my mom, "different" meant "unacceptable".

My eyes started leaking and I could feel my face getting hot and swollen as I tried to hold in my screaming, boiling rage, and helplessness.

I wanted to tell my mother all of these things but I couldn't. It was one of the things I had to work on in therapy with Dr Khan, I guess, expressing the feelings I had bottled up inside of me. But that was for another day. Today, I just wanted to scream.

Jillian's hand was cool around mine. She didn't say anything but seemed to communicate through touch: *it's okay*.

I took deep, gulping breaths as the tears rolled slowly down my hot face. "I don't want to go home," I said. "I just don't want to go home."

My mother was getting angrier by the second, especially after Jillian took my hand.

"Child, whether you like it or not you are going home with me when I leave here. You have a week to resign yourself to the fact that, whether you want to or not, you are going home."

I felt like I did when I was little, the time I tried to hurt her with a knife. I wanted to hurt her. I didn't have a knife but I had my tongue.

"I hate you! I wish I had died when I took those pills, just so I wouldn't have to live with you ever again!" I sobbed. And, jerking my hand from Jillian's cool grasp, I ran to my room and locked the door.

A few minutes later I heard the tapping on my door. From the light touch I knew it could only be Julie. My mother would have banged on the door with a clenched fist; Jillian would have had louder taps. But these taps sounded just like Julie: kind of delicate, but not weak. "Muffin, open the door," she called.

I was in the midst of my enraged tantrum and couldn't move if I tried. Over the sobbing and screaming, I could hear her persistent knocking. After a while I had wound down enough to get up and open the door to her.

She didn't look happy. "Hey. You going to be okay?"

I nodded, still gulping and weeping.

"Then get out there and apologise to your mother. You've really hurt her feelings. I know you're sick but that doesn't give you the excuse to be so rude. I know you're better trained than what I just saw."

I pushed my lips together into a pout my mother called a *swell-face*, turned my back to Julie and sat down hard on my bed. "She is so evil," I sobbed. "She doesn't understand me and she doesn't want to even try. She'll never want me to be happy."

"Be that as it may," Julie responded, implacable, "you still can't talk to your mother any old way. She's your mother and deserves a measure of respect."

Stubbornly, and still crying, I sat and looked at the white eyelet cotton of the comforter on my bed.

"This is not negotiable," Julie said, as softly and as firmly as she had knocked on my door.

I got up, not looking at her, and walked out to the deck. Even before I hit the back door I could hear the raised voices of my mother and Jillian, tossing angry words back and forth like the birdie in badminton.

"…my daughter!" screamed my mother.

"…bad mother!" rejoined Jillian.

"…had no choice!" That was Mom.

"…always have a choice!" That was Jillian.

Without hearing all their words, I knew somehow they were arguing about who was going to keep me. I felt weird, like a toy being fought over by children in a playground.

Their voices dropped for a second and I took the opportunity to walk into the conversation.

"I'm sorry, Mom," I said, without preamble.

"You should be. How dare you talk to me like that?" No easy

apology where Cynthia was concerned, no siree. I had to suffer for my arrogance.

"I don't know what I was thinking," I said, but the sarcasm flew over her head.

"No, I don't think you were thinking at all. You don't talk to me like that, ever. You understand?"

I nodded. I was starting to cry again. I turned around and went back into the house, leaving them staring at my back. Dr Khan would have a field day with this episode, I thought.

"Look, you see how you have her rude rude so!" my mother accused Jillian as soon as the door was shut behind me.

"Me!" Jillian sputtered. "She never talk to me so a day in she life! I never see she get vex once yet in the two months she here..."

Back in my room, Julie was waiting for me.

"I feel like a slave," I told her. "Like I'm on an auction block and the two of them are bidding for me with love instead of money. Who loves me more."

Julie carefully weighed her words before replying. "I don't think it's love, sweetie. Your mother... well, she has a lot of things to offer you. This isn't about love, really. It's not in question who could love you more."

The cryptic words didn't answer any of the unspoken questions I had buzzing around inside of me. What did she mean? Was she saying my mother really didn't love me? That Jillian actually did love me more? Or was she saying that my mother loved me more but that love wasn't all that was required to take care of me?

"I don't understand, Julie. What do you mean?"

She sighed and looked troubled. "I think... I think your mom does love you."

It was a relief to hear it. I did have my doubts.

"But she is not good at showing her love. It comes out as criticism. I guess you could blame her family for it, if you have to blame anybody at all." She shrugged, shook her head. "I don't know. I think it was something about how they were raised. When I met Jillian she was so cold and locked away… it was very hard to get her to admit her feelings about anything. I think your mom is bad at showing her emotions. Believe me, Jillian knew nothing about hugging and saying 'I love you' when we first met. Give Cynthia time."

"Time? She's had me for fourteen years and she still doesn't love me!"

Julie was firm as she corrected me. "Cynthia does love you. That much I do know. But you're sick right now and you need a lot more attention than Cynthia gives you. I don't know if she even knows how to give anybody the kind of loving care you need. She's just… she's just not wired that way." She had used just the words I did when I considered my mom and my illness. I was wired different to Mom, and that was one of the big obstacles between us. She wouldn't ever understand me or accept me.

I told Julie my fears.

She nodded slowly. Her eyes were getting a bit shiny now, too. "Yes, I see what you mean. It is hard for us, too, to deal with your illness. But we are willing to try. I don't think Cynthia is. I really don't. She had you when she wasn't expecting to. From what Jillian tells me, your mom was never very maternal."

"So why did she have me, then?" I scowled.

"You think it's that easy to abort a baby?" Julie asked softly. "Back then it wasn't easy to get an abortion in Trinidad. It still isn't, from what I've seen on Facebook. And you know your mom is Catholic.

That's not something she even considered, Jillian said. Your grandmother would have had a cow."

I considered this. I thought about the rumours about a girl in my school who had disappeared for months and then returned. The ugly things people said about her, even though many of them were also having sex and could have well been in her position. My mother had had me just after leaving secondary school. Come to think of it, she had only been a few years older than I was now. The thought of myself trying to take care of an infant on my own at such a young age was terrifying. I shuddered, the enormity of the burden occurring to me for the very first time.

"I ruined her life," I despaired.

"Oh, no, honey!" Julie hugged me quickly. "Not at all. But you did make it more challenging. And maybe she didn't deal with it so gracefully, but she did the best she could."

The heaviness of the idea of what having me must have meant to my mother's life, her opportunities, her choices weighed on me. It was something I'd definitely have to take to Dr Khan in therapy.

"But I want you to promise me," Julie said, "no matter what happens, that you'll keep an open mind and an open heart. And if you have to go back home, you'll try to give your mom a break."

It was ironic to hear the words, but I understood what they meant. My mom couldn't really handle my illness; I'd have to do it by myself—with doctors, of course. But she wouldn't be as supportive as she should. It wouldn't be the end of the world, but it would make my therapy much harder. One of the things I'd come to love about my home in Edmonton was the unspoken support Jillian and Julie gave to me. It was there in the hugs and the occasional questions: *Are you okay? Is there anything going on we need to talk about?* The glances they gave me were just rich with love and affection. I didn't feel appraised when I walked into a room where they were, just appreciated.

I was dying to ask how come she and Jillian were fighting to keep me, but I didn't want to let Julie know I had overheard her private conversation about having a baby. Finally my curiosity won out.

"Did you and Auntie Jillian talk about keeping me? I guess it wasn't a surprise when my mom came to take me home, since you were so prepared with your arguments."

"It was kind of a surprise," she admitted. "We knew she'd come but didn't expect her until the end of August. I guess she felt we were letting things get out of hand when you had that last breakdown."

Her frank use of the word jarred. I still felt sensitive about my excursion into my mental wasteland; the word "breakdown" was one I'd mentally tiptoed around without actually using it. But when you came down to it, that's what it was. A breakdown. No shame in it, just a need to prevent it from happening again, or, if it did, to make sure it was dealt with in the right way.

"Jillian really wants to have children but I don't think we need to try to do that right now," Julie said, frankly. "We're trying to start a new business, we're breaking even but not really making much money yet… it's not a good time for that."

I tilted my head and looked at her. "How is it okay for me to stay but not okay for you to have a baby?"

Julie grinned. "I don't have to change your diapers, do I?"

I had to laugh in return.

"Can you imagine Jillian doing it? Since I'm the one who'll really be doing the fun stuff like that, I guess I have some say in when we have a baby."

I could see her point.

She was fingering the end of her long ponytail when another, firmer tap came from the door.

It was my mother. Her eyes were red. She looked at Julie and said, "Do you mind if you and I have a word outside?"

Julie nodded and left with Mom.

I waited nervously but didn't have long to wait.

When Julie came in, her wide smile told me all I needed to know.

I was staying.

Chapter
10

Dr Khan gave me an exercise to do. He said I had to make a list of all the things I loved about Trinidad and all the things I hated about it, and all the things I loved about Edmonton and all the things I hated about it. It would help me to process this new stage in my life, he said, because even though I thought I only hated home, nothing is ever that simple.

I started with Trinidad. The things I loved: my mom; Akilah; the sunshine; the beach. It was a short list. The things I hated: my mom; school; how small-minded people were, how judgmental. Things I loved about Edmonton: Jillian and Julie; my bedroom; the library; summer flowers; Joshua. What I hated about Edmonton: everything was so strange, so big and so intimidating, and sometimes I was the only person in the room who looked like me.

Dr Khan looked thoughtful when he saw my list. "You're going to work on this, okay? This is just the tip of the iceberg. Spend some time thinking about what you really miss about home, and what you really like about here. Trust me, it will help you over the next few months. Living here, going to school, it's going to be an adjustment."

Having to give up her only child—even one she had mixed feelings about—wasn't something my mom agreed to lightly. There were terms and conditions. I had to go to school. I had to go home for Christmas. And most of all, I had to swear I was returning to Trinidad at the end of a year.

I would have agreed to anything short of the amputation of my limbs just to hear that I could stay. I anxiously agreed to all her conditions.

The arrangement did nothing for her temperament. Cynthia was sour and distant for the next five days, which was as long as her visit lasted. Even on the four-hour drive to Banff, a national park with the biggest rivers, lakes and mountains I'd ever seen, she sat unimpressed and silent. After a joyless hour of hiking from the pretty little town up the side of a mountain, Julie and Jillian gave up on trying to delight her. The drive back was as silent as the drive there.

On the night before she left, Jillian threw her a dinner party to send her back home. Josh and his dad came.

"Mom," I said, nervously, "this is Joshua. He's Jillian's godson."

She gave him a long up and down look, trying to peer past his skinny jeans and fitted T-shirt to see his soul. I could have told her it wouldn't work, and that she shouldn't judge this book by its cover.

"She's letting you stay?" he said under his breath when we went to the kitchen.

"Yeah," I replied.

"Only for a year, though." I snuck a look at him out the corner of my eye. "What about you?"

"I'm staying!" He was glowing like a light bulb. "My mom isn't exactly thrilled but she's willing to give me up for a year, too. So you'll have company." He laughed shortly but not unkindly. "Dysfunctions R Us..."

Julie had gone all out for this dinner. I was glad. In a way, it was not only my mom's farewell party; it was my welcome home party, too. In the dining room, I looked at the faces reflected in the yellow candlelight. Nathan—drinking a glass of water, I was happy to note— looked peaceful and interested in something my mother was saying.

Jillian looked glad, smiling broadly and proudly. Julie, as usual, looked placid and kind. And Joshua looked excited and thrilled. My mother wasn't happy, I could see. She was frowning, her lips tight and turned down. But as the night wore on I could see her relax somewhat, perhaps getting used to the idea that for the next year she'd be free of the responsibility of having a teenaged daughter tying her down.

I wondered how I looked to them. I could guess: a little anxious, a little excited, plenty hopeful. I had a year to find my feet in this world, a year to get used to my condition. A year to start to get better. I was ready.

I slipped into the tiny closet behind the front door where the coats were kept. I put my hand into the pocket of my Princess Di coat and took out the schedules for the Fourteen bus and the Eighteen bus, the schedules that had been my constant companions since I had come to Edmonton. I crumpled them into balls and took them to the kitchen, where I dumped them into the garbage. Julie was in there to get a fresh bottle of wine. "What's that?" she asked.

"Nothing important," I said. And it was true. I knew my buses. I could find my way home. *Home home was right here.*

From the dining room, Jillian called, "Kayla! Time to eat!"

"Coming!" I answered. Julie took my hand and we walked outside together.

Acknowledgements

I am grateful to God for this opportunity to write about some of his more misunderstood children, and to L.D. for graciously allowing me to use aspects of her personal story here.

Thanks to the team at the CODE Burt Award for Caribbean Young Adult Literature, which caused this book to be published. Thanks to Polly Pattullo and Papillote Press for your patience and kindness.

Thanks to the team of the Bocas Lit Fest, who have done so much for the development and support of Caribbean writers and publishing. Special thanks to Nick Laughlin: your work changes lives.

Thanks to my family and particularly my daughters Ishara and Najja, my nephew Taye, and my husband Brian for their endless love and care for me when I cannot care for myself.